BBC NATIONAL SHORT STORY AWARD 2021

BBC

National
Short Story
Award 2021

with Cambridge University

First published in Great Britain in 2021 by Comma Press.
www.commapress.co.uk

'All the People Were Mean and Bad' by Lucy Caldwell was first published in *Intimacies* (Faber & Faber, 2021). 'Maykopsky District, Adyghe Oblast' by Richard Symth was first published online by TSS Publishing (2021).

A CIP catalogue record of this book is available from the British Library.

ISBN-10: 1-912697-49-1
ISBN-13: 978-1-91269-749-6

The publisher gratefully acknowledges the support of Arts Council England.

Printed and bound in Great Britain by Clays Ltd, Elcograf S.p.A

Contents

Introduction

THE SHORT STORY IS a precise, demanding and sometimes elusive art form. The narrative has to be more concentrated than a novel and more elastic than a poem. It has to be true and of itself; specific, controlled and naturally the right length. So, what should we look for?

Perhaps it is an epiphany, an unforgettable meeting, a defining memory, or a prescient vision of the future. Often, it is something that we couldn't possibly have imagined, a different way of looking at the world so that everything seems a little different once the story has reached its end. Our perceptions tilt.

The pandemic changed life for everyone in 2020. We were 'cabined, cribbed, confined' and became necessarily less social and more reflective. People read more and they wrote more. But what about?

There were several recurrent themes in the

submissions for the 2021 BBC National Short Story Award with Cambridge University. These offer a unique insight into the annual preoccupations of the nation. The familiar subjects of memory and desire were accompanied by intense introspection, a determination to make sense of who we are and how we got here. What is the nature of personal and political identity?

There was longing, too: a craving to imagine journeys into the past and across the globe to escape lockdown. The persistence and unpredictability of a global virus also led to inevitable fears about the future, human extinction and the nightmare of an eco-dystopia.

Anxiety and restlessness were never far away. Perhaps this was a reflection of a world turned in on itself, a fear of triviality and of writers afraid of being 'merely entertaining'. But it was worrying. There were few laughs and it was sad to experience so little hope, redemption or joy. The stories submitted for this award may only be snapshots of the way we live now, but sometimes I longed for a less cautious and more liberated creative momentum, a broader vision of a place outside ourselves: a glimpse of the transcendent.

This made our search for the final five stories even more urgent. We, too, wanted to escape the gloom, to be taken away and transported by a writer's imagination.

Every single piece, including the final shortlisting, was read without us knowing the name, gender or background of the author. The five judges were relative strangers. I only knew Di Speirs, the Books Editor of BBC Radio (a.k.a. the BBC's 'Queen of Books') from my time as Commissioning Editor of Arts at BBC Radio 4. I had never met my other colleagues: Fiona Mozley, whose first novel *Elmet* was shortlisted for the 2017 Booker Prize; Derek Owusu, whose novel *That Reminds Me* won the Desmond Elliott Prize for debut fiction in 2020; and the novelist and short-story writer Donal Ryan, who has won numerous awards and whose book *The Spinning Heart* was recently voted 'Irish Book of the Decade'.

In a way, we still haven't met each other, because our Covid-influenced meetings were all held via Zoom. I think this made the judging all the more impartial. We could never mutate into a literary clique in which we harbour grudges and plot to ruin our rivals. We were watchful of what we thought and said, another sign of the times, and keen to respect each other's opinions and reach consensus. Although we all had our favourites, we soon realised that any of the five authors in this collection could go on to win the ultimate prize.

What we cared about most was the quality of the writing: confidence and originality of tone, acuteness of observation, sharpness of dialogue. We considered the mechanics of storytelling: from the announcement of a first paragraph to the difference between an open and closed ending. We wondered why some of the writing seemed to strive too hard to make an impression (too many adjectives, too much description) while other stories were under-written and did not develop as much as they could have done.

Once we had made sure that the world created in our long shortlist of stories was both authoritative and believable, we considered stylistic details: anything from the shape of a paragraph to the rhythm of a sentence or the fall of a particular word.

We were particularly struck by Lucy Caldwell's 'All the People Were Mean and Bad', an assured and tender account of a transatlantic aeroplane encounter between a young mother, her small child and the man in the next-door seat. The narrative contains no false notes, is alive to different possibilities, and negotiates the gap between what is thought with what is actually said and done with consummate skill. The story has a taut, accumulative power and has so many perceptive observations about love, responsibility, and the impossible possibility of an alternate life.

We were thrilled by the freshness and energy in the description of a locker-room full of adolescent Irish boys in Rory Gleeson's 'The Body Audit'. This is a story told with vigorous intimacy in which insecurity and anxiety can be trumped by febrile optimism and unexpected kindness.

We were moved by Georgina Harding's 'Night Train', in which two very different women meet on a journey to Kiev and talk through the night about history, loss, quilts, shawls and defiance. The narrative rhythm beautifully mirrors the pace of the train and the story has all the pull and texture of dream.

Danny Rhodes's 'Toadstone' contrasts health with sickness, memory and the present, duty with serendipity, uniformity with difference and the banal with the profound. It is subtle and wistful and seems to ask nothing less than what really makes up a life. It also has a stunningly beautiful final paragraph.

And finally, we were intrigued by the loaded and watchful conversation in Richard Smyth's eerie tale of surveillance set in Stalin's Soviet Union in 1949: 'Maykopsky District, Adyghe

Oblast'. This narrative, like all the others, contains such skill in the telling, that it makes you want to re-read it straight away to work out how its effects are achieved.

Like all the best fiction, these tales take the reader into a sharply different and distilled world. All of them will be read aloud, as great stories should be, on BBC Radio 4, which has been the home of this particular form of storytelling for the last seven decades.

I hope that you, the reader, enjoy them as much as we have done. It has been a privilege to evaluate and celebrate works of fiction that increase our understanding of ourselves and each other. All these stories cast a discerning eye over what it is to be human and what it means to be vulnerable. They understand the importance of kindness, the horror of cruelty and the power of the imagination to define what it means to be alive. Like all the finest literature, they are a call to live life intensely; to define, investigate and understand it as much as we can; and to appreciate our flickering humanity as bravely as we dare.

James Runcie,
London, 2021

All the People Were Mean and Bad

Lucy Caldwell

Two weeks after your cousin dies, you're on a night flight back to London from Toronto. Your daughter, at 21 months, too young for her own seat, but too old, really, to be on your lap, is overtired and restless. Your phone battery is dead. With no more cartoons, all you have to entertain her while the plane taxis and waits, taxis and waits, inching towards the runway and its take-off slot, is the book your aunty gave her as you were leaving, a book from your aunty's church. It's the story of Noah's Ark, illustrated for pre-schoolers, the first in a series self-funded and published by the church.

All the people, it says, *were mean and bad. Except for Noah.*

Noah was good, and because he was good, God saved him.

You hate this book.

Shall we look at the animals now? you say,
but your daughter says, No. She likes the animals,
but she likes these pages even better. Over a
whole double-page spread, the mean and bad
people are doing mean and bad things: pulling
each other's hair and laughing, aiming slingshots
and catapults at each other, gurning and scowling
and spitting and stamping their feet. You point at
each of them in turn, naming their misdemeanours,
and your daughter makes extravagant faces and
laughs with delight.

Ok, let's look at the animals, you say firmly, and
turn the page, but your daughter throws back her
head and wails.

I'm sorry, you say to the man sitting next to
you – the man who has the misfortune to be
sitting next to you, for the remaining seven
hours and 36 minutes of this flight; the only,
admittedly small, consolation being it's a whole
half-hour shorter than on the way there.

No problem, he says, and he starts to say,
again, and unnecessarily, because he's already
been too kind to you, lifting your bags up into
the overhead locker and fetching beakers and
bunnies and bribes of white chocolate buttons
and finally the book from the stuffed chaotic tote
at your feet, even getting up to ask the stewardess

to rinse out a bottle for you in the galley, that he understands, has children himself, two sons – but the pitch of your daughter's cry is rising. You grimace an apology at him, and he smiles back then looks tactfully away, as if there's nothing to see at all.

Please, you say to your daughter, red-faced now and howling, Please, come on, Matilda, shh, and you suppress the urge to shake her, or start howling yourself, and you turn back and take a deep breath and begin again: *All the people were mean and bad.*

There is one page in the book that you like: a page of blue, just blue, with a tiny Ark in the very top right-hand corner.

No words, nothing, just the sudden giddy perspective; the weight of all the fallen rain. It is, you think, the only truthful picture in the whole story.

Your daughter wriggles and cries for the whole ascent, but as the plane reaches cruising altitude, and the seat-belt sign pings off, and the in-flight cabin service begins, she finally falls asleep on your chest and you hold her, heavy and warm and limp and sprawling, and as her breathing shudders and lengthens you let your own eyes close. Seven hours and three minutes left. Just a little over three thousand miles. It seems more than time and distance you're traversing. It is a lifetime ago that you left London. And it will be one of the longest stretches you and your husband have ever been apart; by far the longest he's not seen Tilly.

You went with him on a couple of shoots after Tilly was born: one to Dublin, another to Cape Town. But it wasn't what either of you had thought it would be and it certainly wasn't a holiday, trying to placate a baby in unfamiliar surroundings, endless hours wandering alone or lying in a hotel room trying to sleep while half-waiting for him to come back. A driver, each time, at your disposal, but where to drive to, and when you got there, what to do? It was, in the end, far lonelier than being at home alone with Tilly would have been, and after those two trips, you didn't do it again.

You think of times apart early on, when you, or usually he, would be away, and of meeting each other again, at train stations or getting out of taxis, and how strange and shy you'd feel, wondering if he'd look different to how you remembered him, or smell wrong, and how sometimes, at first, you could barely look him in the eye. You've tried, for Tilly's sake, to talk every day: Cape Town is six hours ahead of Toronto, so you FaceTimed each night at her bedtime, his midnight, but he was inevitably still up, either drinking with the crew or trying to resolve more problems on an already fraught and overextended shoot.

You are trying not to think of it, this prolonged separation, as a separation, as a test.

Anything for your wife? the stewardess's voice says, and you open your eyes.

Oh, you say, we're not – just as he says, Oh, we're not – and he grins.

I think, he says, she needs a gin and tonic too? and you smile and say, Yes, thank you, that sounds good, and the stewardess scoops the ice and drops in lemon and opens the little green bottle and flips the can's tab with deft, practised movements, and he takes it from her and sets it on the tray table next to his.

Thank you, you say again, and you shift your daughter's weight to free a hand and take the cup from him.

Cheers, he says, the twang of his accent making it almost two syllables, like yours, and you reply with your almost two syllables, Cheers, and you touch cups and sip.

To sleeping babies, he says, and you say, Look, I'm so sorry, and he says, I once flew solo with the twins when they'd just turned three,

Vancouver to Sydney, with a layover in LA, oh boy.

Solo with twins, you say, and he says, Yeah, my wife was away and the childminder was sick, it was like a bad farce, I wouldn't wish that journey on anyone, and he's quiet for a moment and says, My sister died an hour before we got there, and then he says, Sorry.

My cousin just died, you say, and I hadn't seen her in years, but for a while, she was like a sister to me.

I'm sorry, he says, at the same time you say, Sorry, too, because a cousin you haven't spoken to in years is not the same as a sister, and even if there's no real metric to grief, there is, must be, a hierarchy of loss.

You touch cups again, sombrely this time, and sip, and finally break eye contact and look away, and neither of you says anything for a while, until he says, That's twenty years ago now, and you say nothing, because what is there to say?

The blazing sunshine and high blue skies, t-shirt weather, the leaves just turning on the trees, a stupidly perfect day. The cool and calm of the mortuary chapel, old for Toronto, designed and built, you read, by John G. Howard in 1842. White brick and Georgetown stone, deep-set trefoil windows and the steeply pitched roof; a fine example of Gothic Revival architecture in Canada. In the little vestibule, the tinny bluegrass of *Hey Duggee* from your phone as the squirrels arrived again and again at the clubhouse to bake carrot cakes for the stoner bunnies; Roly, the excitable little hippo, and Happy, the crocodile with his adoptive elephant parents, Betty the octopus rocking up in her dad's little orange submarine, Norrie the mouse and Tag the rhino, all leaping up, to Tilly's delight, for their Duggee-hug; while in the nave the priest intoned and the mourners responded, standing and sitting and singing and weeping, and your cousin was no more.

We are all ashes and dust eventually, you think, but now she already was: her warm taut body, pressed next to yours in your sleeping bags zipped together, as she confided about a boy she'd kissed; her long brown legs in their blue shorts with the red piping taking the stairs two and three at a time, the tattoos she tried to give you both when you were twelve and she was fourteen with the spike of her compass and a cartridge of ink from your yellow Parker fountain pen, below your hipbone where neither of your mothers would see it, and where a smudge of blue dots still remains.

You think of all of this and you think how impossible it is that all of it's gone; how the fact of its being gone makes none of it, nothing, feel true anymore, not that people can ever really know each other, or truly love, or that it matters in the end if a marriage fails, or ever could have worked; and yet how can it all not matter?

The meals trolley has made its way to you. Your tray table doesn't fold down over your daughter's sleeping body, so he takes your meal on his too, arranges both little trays lengthwise.

Shall I cut it up for you? he says, and you laugh in embarrassment as he tears and butters your bread roll, forks up cubes of chicken, the way you might for Tilly.

You don't manage more than a few bites before it all becomes too much – the bizarre intimacy of this stranger feeding you.

I'm fine, you say, I'm actually not that hungry, and it's true, you haven't been for a while, and not just because of the jet lag, or since the initial shock of your cousin's death, but for weeks now, maybe even months. You know you're getting thin, and you've brushed it off and blamed it on running after a toddler, and you've made an effort, for her as much as for you, to make yourself eat. But the hollow feeling at your centre, the ache in your solar plexus, voids all hunger, and it feels somehow right to be at a light-headed remove from the world, this sense of being vague, and insubstantial, as if you could just drift on, indefinitely; as if you don't really exist, or need to. Sometimes, you think, your daughter is the only person who feels real, because the immediacy of her needs is so urgently, incontrovertibly so.

So what do you do, he's saying, as if he's reading your mind, or are you a full-time mom? and you're saying, No, I'm an architect, then qualifying it with, at least I used to be, because what, actually, do you do now with your days, beyond endlessly push a buggy round the city streets, taking photographs, not even with your SLR, just screens' and screens' worth of photos on your phone, stone detailing or glazed-brick facades, ghost signage or board-marked concrete, large Queen Anne sash windows or tiny Huguenot busts to hold shutters in place, not even for any reason, you've even stopped bothering to upload them to your laptop any more.

From November, you say, when Tilly turns two, you'll have the nursery place: three mornings a week to begin with, then when she settles, the afternoon sessions too. Your husband says you should take on some private resi. Leaflet the neighbours. Loft conversions or extensions, something to keep you busy, get you working again. He's begun to say lately that you could set up your own practice, as if he doesn't know the first thing about architecture, despite being married to you all these years. But at the same time, he's sort of right: what else are you going to do with your days?

He nods, listening, and you find yourself talking on.

Another baby would of course be the logical thing, and as an only child yourself, you badly want Tilly to have a brother or sister; and yet. Every time you have the discussion, about babies, or work, about what happens next, you feel deeply tired; an exhaustion that seeps into, or maybe from, your very bones. Bone-weary: you used to feel a sort of delight when a word or a phrase was a perfect fit, the mathematical logic of it; but now, for the first time in your life, you just feel old.

You stop, abruptly, expecting him to laugh at that, but he doesn't laugh.

I'm 56, he says, which on a bad day rounds up to 60, and I'm two years divorced, and my boys are almost 24.

You realise you've been trying to work out his age.

Fifty-six, you say, not meaning to say it aloud, and he puts up his hands and winces.

I'm not, he says, I know I'm not, but in so many ways I still feel 24 myself.

I know what you mean, you say. I mean, I don't feel any different, I don't think, than I did then?

I don't think, he says, we ever really do.

You don't think people change, you say, or ever really can?

I think people change, he says, for sure, but only ever become, essentially, more themselves.

You don't know if that thought is comforting or profoundly sad.

Then where's the hope, you say, if we can never truly begin again, or become, I don't know, something else or better?

He shrugs, and smiles. Each moment, I guess, he says.

Each moment, here now, that's what we have. That's what we have, or that's all we have? Perhaps it's both.

A girl you were at university with had married a man 25 years older, more, technically, than twice her age: she 24, he 49. She'd been engaged before that to a guy from uni; he'd been a Blue and they were something of a golden couple. No one could understand it. You didn't know her very well, but you somehow once got drunk together and she started crying and said the loneliest thing in the world was lying in bed with someone and wanting someone else's hands to be on you instead.

They had a daughter whom they'd had almost immediately, long before any of your other uni friends had kids, who must be in her teens by now. After that drunken night, you'd stayed in touch for a while, and bought a present when the baby was born, a ruffled pinafore from a place whose clothes cost as much as adult clothes, and came, in a sort of performance by the cashier, wrapped in palest lemon tissue.

That was the only time you'd been to their house, because you felt so awkward there. They had peonies in vases, and Le Creuset pans, and a magnetic knife rack with proper, monogrammed knives, and different-sized wine glasses for white or red, and acres of white linen on the huge bed you passed on the way to the baby's room, and the guest bathroom, with its cut-grass scented soap. The house, in retrospect, wasn't that remarkable – just a modest terrace on a street in Kentish Town – but it felt at the time like being at someone's posh English parents', and you'd thought how strange it was that this, now, was her life, a quantum leap away from bedsits and flatshares and badly carved-up Victorian houses and boxy shared-ownership starter flats.

But what struck and maybe discomfited you most was how devoted she was to him: as if, after all they'd done, there wasn't the luxury of being anything else – exasperated or bickering. It had seemed to you an exhausting way of living; although you wonder now if maybe it wasn't that at all, but rather the knowledge that they'd found each other too late in life, or in his life at least, to be reckless, or casual; that the way they loved was careful and tender not because they didn't, but because they did love each other with a sort of abandon.

You have Riedel wine glasses and Dartington Crystal champagne flutes yourself now, and Japanese knives and a proper knife-sharpener, and sometimes even peonies in vases, or at least in a vase. Where has it all come from? How have you graduated, almost without noticing, from novelty shot glasses and wine glasses nicked from pubs, thick-rimmed and engraved with measures, to this? How have you come so far from your Pioneer parents, their bottle of Shloer at Christmastime or weddings, the single blue bottle of Harveys Bristol Cream they kept as a concession to your grandma? A wedding of your own; a marriage to a producer with extravagant Christmas and birthday and anniversary tastes. And yet: you can't shake the sense that it has all crept up on you without your wanting or asking for it, without your feeling any different than you did at 29, 27, or, yes, 24.

Can I ask you something? he says, and you say, inexplicably flustered, Sure.

He picks up the book, which has fallen to the floor, and opens it.

Do you really believe in – well, that? he says. That people are mean and bad, and – for want of a better word – damned?

He looks at the mean and bad people for a moment before closing the book and reaching to slide it back into your tote bag.

I was brought up believing it all, you say. God and Noah, the Flood, the Ark – I was brought up believing it was literal truth. That the world was six thousand years old and the Devil had planted fossils to try to trick us.

So that sounds like you no longer believe it.

Your aunty: pale-faced, her hair drawn back to show new cheekbones, gaunt, but lit with the belief that your cousin was finally in a better place. The way the priest talked about the prescription drugs as her demons. The flights of

14

angels that would have been there for her at the end.

I sometimes think it would be easier if I still did.

That's why you read it to your daughter?

Oh no, you say. No! I'm not – I'm going to tactically misplace the book as soon as we get home. My aunty just gave it to her. It's something to read – that's all.

I guess I'd like to think, he says, that people are basically good.

Neither of you says anything for a while.

I'd love to be able to live like that, you say, and just for a moment it feels like a weight is lifting.

Your daughter wakes. Her ears are sore, and she doesn't understand it. You've used your last carton of milk. He goes to the galley and comes back with a handful of UHT sticks which he tears and empties, one by one, into her bottle, the millilitres accumulating until there's enough for her to drink. While he does this, you pace with her, joggle her, up and down the cabin, and although the lights are dimmed now and most people are sleeping, or attempting to, no one looks at you angrily. When the bottle is filled enough, he holds Tilly while you go to the loo. In the little metal room, you splash water on your face and think: *I must do better. I must start eating again, and make a plan for what happens next.*

Even when Tilly sleeps again, you don't, and nor does he. You both watch the minute, ticking progress of the little blue plane icon, over the emptiness of the North Atlantic Ocean, its route curving up towards Greenland and the Labrador Sea before it will begin to fall again towards Ireland and onwards and home, endless, inexorable. You watch it, and talk some more, and these are some of the things you talk about. How unfeasible it is that this great sleek lumbering mass of metal can rise instead of falling, into the sky, up and up, can traverse the globe along invisible, predetermined tracks, corridors in the air, while its passengers sleep and watch films and flush toilets and request more ice for their gin and tonic and eat bread rolls specially engineered to taste normal at low pressure and in dry cabin air. That there is the world, the ocean, the dark roiling waves, thirty, however many thousand feet beneath, and here you are, suspended above it all, hurtling onwards at hundreds of miles an hour into the dawn of an entirely different day. How time as a measure is, for a while, entirely meaningless, in this time out of time, and how distance is too, and about the

distances we travel, between where we come
from and where we end up, between who we
thought we were and who we turn out to be.
About how – who knows? – for your daughter,
there will not be transatlantic travel, at least not
like this, and it may seem the most grotesque
decadence of a bygone age. We think, or rather
we live – or at least you do, or have – as if things
will continue forever, and we so rarely talk about
the only things, in hindsight, that matter. All of
these words, these thousands of words, and none
of them the right ones, the handful of words that
might have meant or even changed something.
And, once again, only this time with even more
urgency, *can* people change, or is it already too
late, is it always too late? Or is there always
another brief window in which anything is
possible?

And these are just some of the things.

The plane descends. Tray tables and seat backs,
seat belts, final cabin checks. Blurs of light
resolving themselves into constellated pinpoints;
buildings, roads, almost individual head-lamps.
The rattle and grind of the landing gears, the
final roar of the engines. The headlong rush of
the plane onto tarmac, the shuddering certainty
of it. Your stomach lurching.

He carries your bags for you off the plane as you carry Tilly, still heavy with sleep. You wait together as they fetch the buggy, and you kick and yank it upright, and strap Tilly in. By this stage, you're among the last off the plane, and several other red-eye flights have come in too, and the Immigration Hall is packed.

Oh no, you say, and he rests a hand lightly on your shoulder.

Hello, Heathrow, my old friend.

For a moment, you stand there, in the crowd, breathing as one.

Sir, madam, this way, please, a uniformed woman is saying, families this way, and she's sliding open a barrier tape so that you can pass into the Family & Special Assistance lane.

He smiles at you, and you smile back.

Thank you, you say to the uniformed woman.

As you manoeuvre the buggy around and join the other lane, which doesn't seem to be moving any faster, perhaps even slower, he murmurs in your ear, Though whether this is a help or a disincentive for travelling as a family, time alone shall tell.

You pass through Immigration as a family, through Baggage Reclaim, and pause before the sliding doors of the Arrivals hall, where your husband will be meeting you and Tilly: he's timed his flight back from Cape Town to coincide with yours.

So I guess this is it, he says. Are you going to be okay? Yes, you say, because what else can you possibly say?

And you take the handle of your suitcase from him, and you walk, not a family at all but two entirely separate people now, through the final Customs channel; *Nothing to Declare*.

Your husband isn't there.

You find a power socket and plug in your phone. A series of messages: he's been further delayed in Cape Town, the assistant producer couldn't handle it after all, the dancer who's broken her ankle, the problem with insurance, the sequence that needs to be reshot. He had to turn back halfway to the airport to deal with it all. He's not now going to be home until tomorrow, or maybe the next day, he won't know until tonight. He's going to make it up to you. Love to Tilly. Tell her he's got the biggest present for her. Take a cab!

You knew it, you thought. Even as he was texting you as you boarded the flight in Toronto, saying he was on his way to the airport too, you knew and dreaded this.

You hold down the button until your phone goes dark again.

He stays with the buggy and bags and the charging phone while you go, Tilly grizzling on your hip, to rinse out the bottle in a sink in the loos then beg some warm milk from the Costa. You could do with a coffee yourself, and should have offered to get him one, but you don't have enough hands. You think of your mother: her jokes about needing a spare pair of hands, her claim to have eyes in the back of her head that you and your cousin once combed her hair repeatedly to disprove. Your mother would have been younger than you are now. You and your cousin just a handful of years from your daughter.

It goes, all of it, and then it's just – gone.

But here you are, now. The chaotic, impatient bustle of Heathrow Arrivals, all the milling, surging, purposeful, harried people. Seven seventeen in the morning, a September Tuesday.

Tilly, strapped back in the buggy, draining her milk, temporarily quiet.

Right, you say, and take the handle of your case again.

Okay.

Let me give you a lift, he says, there'll be a driver for me, a car, I'll see you safely home.

His eyes are very blue.

For a moment, you almost say yes.

You think of the books that you and your

cousin loved, the ones with multiple pathways through, and dozens of endings. You'd read them lying on your stomachs, heads pressed together, holding various pages, options, open. You'd always be careful, trying to make it through, and she'd choose the most reckless routes possible, just to see what might happen. She would have gone with him. You think: If she was still here, at the other end of a WhatsApp stream or the tap of a FaceTime away, she'd say to you, Do it.

But no, you hear yourself saying, it will be easier with your daughter on the train, she's been cooped up so long, at least in a train you can walk up and down, and besides, she gets carsick. The train to Paddington, then, and then the tube, and maybe a taxi for the last bit, at the very end.

But your bags, and the buggy, he says, how will you manage?

People are helpful, you say, they've been so helpful, every bit of the way – and it's true, you realise in a rush, thinking of the taxi driver who found you a trolley, wheeled your bags into the terminal, right up to the Air Canada desk; of Chantal, who upgraded you to premium economy for free, so you and Tilly would have a bit more room. Her long nails, midnight blue with crystals, tapping, and how, in an attempt to give her something back, you'd said how you admired them, offering up your own short, bitten fingernails, and how she'd beamed. Of the people around you who didn't roll their eyes or glare at you as Tilly howled; and him, of course; and him – and suddenly, you find yourself on the verge of all the tears you haven't yet cried.

Oh, he says, oh, and he says, Come here, and he takes your face in both his hands and brushes away the tears with his thumbs, and then there's a moment, and everything tilts.

Heathrow Arrivals resolves itself back around you. There is an artist whose work you saw once in a Whitechapel gallery: she had stitched to a globe of the world metallic threads representing one single day's flights, then somehow dissolved the globe, leaving just the sugar-spun mass of threads, and you think of it now, of how it made you think, how fine the threads that connect us from one person, or place, to another, and how precious, and how strong.

I have to go, you say, because if you stay for a moment longer, you won't; or won't be able to.

What are you going to do now? he says.

Now this minute now, or now in a more existential sense? you say, and somehow you manage to say it lightly.

He looks at you, then takes up your cue.

Somewhere between the two?

We're going to watch *Hey Duggee* on the train, for as long as the battery lasts. We're going to be home by ten. We're going to press all the buttons in the lift. We're going to do the shopping and maybe bake a cake, which will really be a pretext for cracking lots of eggs and bashing the shells up with a teaspoon.

He laughs. You realise you love that laugh. You love that you've made him laugh. For a moment, nothing else matters.

Okay then, he says, softly, and you hear or maybe feel him take a breath, and let it slowly out. Take it easy.

Take it easy, you say back. Okay, he says. Goodbye.

Goodbye, you say.

You do let Tilly press all of the buttons in the lift, all seven of them, from LG for the car park to the floors beyond your flat. You don't sigh when the slow doors judder open and closed, open and closed. You just feel numb. You do bake the cake. You let Tilly crack the whole carton of eggs, far more than you need, and you think it's ok, you'll make an omelette later. You tell her the joke about Hamlet and egos that your cousin, at thirteen, had to explain to you; and you turn away before she can see that your laughter at how clever you thought it is turning to sobs.

From your little balcony, the September sky is high and cloudless.

You could email him, you think. You didn't swap addresses, but you could google his name, his company. You won't, but you could.

You call up a Google tab on your phone. You won't. You don't.

You look at a map of Canada on your phone instead. It's so vast, is what gets you, there's just so much *space*; the cities of Toronto and Ottawa and Montreal and then Quebec City in a tidy row just up from New York state and the US border; and above them the open space of Ontario and Quebec and Newfoundland and Labrador; and westwards beyond that the breadth of Manitoba and Saskatchewan and British Columbia; Vancouver, where he was born and lived for the two and a half decades of his marriage, and northwards of it the Yukon and the Northwest Territories and Nunavut, the whole sweep of it, so empty, so much, that you have to hold on to the balustrade to steady yourself, on the verge of doubling over with a sort of homesickness, this sudden intensity of loss.

Breathe, you tell yourself, just breathe.

Your husband is only doing his best. He's

been so worried since Tilly was born and you
stopped work, about providing for you; about
the precariousness of his industry; about what it
means to be a family. He's doing his best and you
think that you must do your best too, to still love
him, and you think that love gone wrong or
astray is also a kind of exile.

It was right, you tell yourself, not to accept
the lift. It would have been a line crossed; some
new frontier, new country, from which you might
not have returned.

And yet.

You wonder, can't help yourself wondering,
what it would have been like had you gone with
him: in his executive car, even back to his hotel,
maybe, where he holds you in his arms; kneels
before you and presses his face to you; eases your
jeans from your hips and unbuttons your shirt
and lays you carefully on his bed; and maybe
that's what you want, for someone to undress
you and lay you down, to make the decisions for
you; but however you try to stage the sequence
in your head, you can't get past the fact of your
daughter there, and the whole thing dissipates.

You try to keep Tilly up until her bedtime, but
she's far too tired, and so you give in mid-
afternoon. It means she'll be wide awake at

midnight, but so, probably, will you. She wants the book, which you have forgotten to lose, but you barely begin it before she's sucking the collar of your lumberjack shirt and has fallen asleep. You lie there for a while before attempting to ease her down, gazing at the cartoon people with their ugly, gargoyle faces. *All the people were mean and bad*, except that what he said is right – they weren't, they couldn't be, that isn't the way you want to live this life, or whatever of it remains to you. They were only doing their best, you think, or the best they thought they could; and unlike stern, righteous, virtuous Noah, no one, ever, told them they were going to die, or be saved, or that any of it, in the end, ever mattered.

The Body Audit

Rory Gleeson

THE ROOM STANK OF boy, of dried sweat and
burps and acne cream and fake aftershave and
mouldy sandwiches and tang, though it was the
whack of old towels that really dominated. They
were littering the room, damp and over-used,
folded over the top rails of bunkbeds and draped
on the backs of chairs and hung from curtain
rods over the PVC windows and heaped near the
door and tangled in piles on the greasy floor.
They'd been deployed to soak up the sweat from
hours of football on the gravel pitch beside the
prefabs, then brought on beach trips to dry
ocean-salted torsos, slung across necks or stuffed
into drawstring bags. If the smell of any one
towel became too much, it received a thorough
spraydown from a can of Lynx Africa, then was
packed tight around a radiator or allowed to flap
outside on the clothesline. Bunk beds lined each

of the three walls, with eight young lads sitting on or beside them, so habituated to the smell they'd created they no longer even sensed it. The fourth wall was taken up by a steamy window that looked out onto the back field, and it was this window the lads were facing. A small area just in front of the window had been cleared of rubbish, ready for the Analysis. It was warm and mildewy in the room, a late sun-shower having taken over outside, as the teenagers eyed each other, and waited for the next sacrifice.

Lorcan was positioned by the door. He had the handle squeezed tight in his palm, holding it up at the highest point of its rotation. If someone tried to enter the room, they'd have to drag the handle all the way down against his resistance, and then force past the barrier of his side-turned foot. If anyone came snooping, either the Bean an Tí Máire, or her husband Dan, or Cinnire Paul, the seventeen-year-old placed in charge of them, off somewhere else in the house texting his new girlfriend, Lorcan's Barrier, as Lorcan called it, would give the occupants of the room time to hide any wrongdoing. Though they were fifteen years old and talked endlessly about war and violence and street fights and their own willingness to perform outrageous sexual acts on human or beast, they were, in behaviour and aspect, naïve and gormless and goodhearted. They were from disparate parts of the country, from Dublin, Westmeath, Limerick, Cork, Donegal. Placed together at random in Tigh Ní Fhlatharta, where despite different interests and a generalised hatred of the learning of the Irish language – their reason for being there – some inexplicable chemistry of hormones and in-group dynamics had brought them close. Strangers two weeks before, they had nicknames now, private jokes, policy differences, rivalries, bullies and fallguys, conflicting ideas about what constituted a great arse. Today though, those things were being put aside. At the end of the second week of their stay together, less than a couple of hours before the Friday disco, they'd decided to finish out their latest ritual.

Lorcan bolstered Lorcan's Barrier, making sure it was secure. He indicated he was ready, then the young men turned their heads as Damien hoisted himself up from his lotus position by the boiler door, and picked his way through the rubbish-strewn floor. He settled in front of the window, facing them.

Let's go, Lorcan said.

Damien's jaw tensed as he pulled his t-shirt off up over his head and held it loosely in one hand down by his side. Each young man watching him noted the particulars of his chest and stomach, his armpits, his elbows, his hands, the height of his belt, the body hair distribution and thickness, the mass, the muscle, the bulk, and weighed their words. In the silence, Damien let the t-shirt drop to the floor. His hand made faint grabbing movements still down by his side, as if he was searching for where he'd dropped it. The grasping of his hand pushed Mango, the least patient of the group, to break the silence from his bottom bunk.

Farmer's tan first of all, he said.

There was a warm hum of agreement. Damien's sunburn was indeed bad. His nuclear-red arms and neck made it look as though he was actually wearing a skin-tight white t-shirt with nipples. Others chipped in from around the room. Lorcan by the door, Vinny on the top bunk.

The red around his neck. Jaysus.

Flat stomach, but his hips are a bit narrow.

Fanning and Tetrapak joined in, the tempo picking up.

He's got points on his shoulders, like, triangles of bone on them.

True. Hardly a problem though.

Nah, just saying like.

Sam circled his forefinger, pointing out critical aesthetic problems.

There's a giant gap between his stomach hair and his chest hair, he said.

At least he has chest hair, came the reply.

You know what I'm saying, Sam said.

All were taking part now, except for Greg, who was keeping silent as he sat behind the laundry basket with his knees crossed. He had one hand under his Black Sabbath t-shirt, surreptitiously playing with a small roll of fat below his ribcage, which bulged larger when he bent forward. He caught Lorcan glancing at him from the door, and so turned his attention full onto Damien.

He's not far off having abs, Greg said.

True, Vinny noted.

Damien didn't know where to put his hands during his judgement. At first he tried for a defiant, hands on hips, arms akimbo position he'd seen in a TedTalk about faking it till you made it, but his hands didn't rest naturally on his hips, so he placed them instead behind his back, fingers loosely intertwined, which dropped his shoulders and stuck out his hips, giving him a more coquettish aspect.

He's standing like a girl.

Give us a curtsy there, Damo.

Take it serious, lads, Lorcan said.

Vinny was lying on his front on the top

bunk, looking down on Damien from on high. Lying on his front was the only way he could think to smother the boner that had sprang up without much warm warning. It was an often enough occurrence, the unexpected boner, so he let it be, feeling its warmth sandwiched between him and the bed. He wriggled forward an inch or two, dragging his boner with him, and slid his chin further onto the guardrail, his head cocked slightly to the side in good judgement. Vinny, known to be confident with women, was seen as a man of taste, a judge of what was fashionable. He could tell you what deodorant was best for inviting a closer sniff, which chat-up lines could lead to further engagement, how to go about soliciting a nude. He'd tell you what to do with your hair, your belt, how fingering worked.

You're skinny, he said. But in a good way. Your ribs are clear under your skin, but not like a neglected baby.

Neglected baby!

You do have sticky-uppy bony bits on your shoulders, but that's not a problem. I'd say you need to add a bit of mass on them all the same anyway.

Damien nodded and squeezed his lips shut. He looked down at himself.

I wish I was stronger.

You're strong enough, lad. You can hold your own if you need to.

Damien was standing a little straighter now. The possibility of a bad reaction or hurtful judgement seemed to have passed, and now he seemed genuinely interested in the perception of his body.

I've good forearms, I think. Veiny.

They're okay, Sam said. Women don't notice forearms so much.

I heard one of the girls from Tigh Neachtain saying she loved Fanning's hands.

In fairness, Fanning has got great hands.

Fanning, sitting on the ground hugging his knees, raised two large, well-defined hands, rotating them this way and that.

I don't see what the big deal is, he said.

Fuck off Fanman, you know you have nice hands.

Lads, back to Damien.

You don't dress for your shape, Vinny said. Or your colour. And you're too stiff. You stand too straight. You're awkward. But that's *attitude*, man. That's not looks.

Damien stood square, his chest widely presented.

Your shoulders *could* do with a bit more muscle, Sam said.

It doesn't matter when you buy good clothes.

You look good in a fitted t-shirt. When it's baggy you look small though.

Don't wear so many long sleeve shirts, dude, they stretch you out.

Honestly lad, you've not much to complain about.

What about his nipples?

What about them?

I mean, they're small.

Small but not tiny small.

They're not big.

No, but they're not noticeably small.

Jesus, lads, Lorcan said. It's a first impression second impression kind of thing. Not a full body scan.

You didn't mind full body scanning me, Sam said.

You should do some more sit-ups, Vinny interrupted. You're skinny so it'd show real well.

Yeah, sit-ups don't do shit if you have a belly.

Back by the laundry basket, Greg smacked his belly through his Sabbath tee a little too hard.

I'm fucked so, he said.

The others ignored the remark, and Mango spoke from his bunk.

Show us your back.

Damien did a slow rotation, showing all sides.

Is that a birthmark on the shoulder blade?

That or a big freckle.

It's a birthmark, Damien said, reaching for it. Is it noticeable?

You'd notice it, but you wouldn't even think about it.

A few seconds elapsed without comment, the energy of the assessment having waned, whereupon Lorcan summed up the diagnosis from the door.

So, you're in good nick, I'd say, generally. You've a good shape, solid proportions. Maybe just do a few sit-ups and stop with the baggier clothes.

Damien took a moment to process this, save the comments for the rest of his life, file them under 'Body Concerns, Teenage, Long-lasting'. He bent and picked up his t-shirt, pulled it back over his head, then went to sit down beside Fanning on the bottom bunk. He sat back against the wall, rubbing his forearms up and down, soothing himself. Fanning leaned over and rapped him on the knee with the knuckles of a well-veined hand.

Well done, Damo.

Cheers, Fanning.

Let's give him a hand so, Lorcan said. Good man, Damien.

Applause went round the room, Damien nodding to each young man from his bunk, showing he was not upset, that he was grateful, then he dropped his head and silently mouthed their comments to himself, word for word, over and over. A grey gloom settled on the evening as the last spits of rain came in a late shower. The room was hot and smelly still, stuffy in the gloom. A radiator had cranked on somewhere and the floor had turned oily and in points sticky with spilled Coke and dried yoghurt. Tension slipped past Lorcan's Barrier and slowly filled the humid room, as the most sensitive case of the evening, Greg, was now up.

Lorcan took up a different position on the door, holding it shut with his hip and using an underhand grip on the handle. He watched Greg, who was sitting behind the basket, waiting for his name to be called. His head was bent and he was looking at his shoes. Lorcan thought about maybe passing him over, forgetting to call his name. But it would be too obvious. Plus, they'd all of them shown themselves, and Greg had commented and opined along with the rest, taken part, and so now it was his turn. He shouldn't be allowed to wuss out.

For Greg, looking at his shoes, gently stretching his Sabbath shirt, this was a moment he'd been dreading for the longest time. He'd always been carrying too much weight, could never in his life have been called skinny, but he felt he'd never completely stepped over the line into full-on Fat Guy status. For the last eighteen months, though, Greg had been at a particularly awkward level of fat, inconsistently and unconventionally shapen. T-shirts either came too tight around him, showing the odd bits of jiggle where some extra fat was deposited, or they came too large and swamped him loose and baggy, making his whole frame loom. He'd developed a stoop in the last year to hide the slight puffy sag of fat about his chest, and to provide increased protection to his extra sensitive nipples. Soon after his fourteenth birthday, they'd become incredibly touchy, such that even a slight knock on an areola caused him excruciating pain. As he and his friends frequently liked to participate in dog piles and wrestling matches, this near-constant Greco-Roman grinding put him in a state of often and sometimes extreme discomfort. The pain in his nipples, along with the sag of his chest, and the relatively imperceptible growth of his penis, had resulted in a genuine fear that he may have missed hitting puberty, or that he had somehow been born with or acquired along the way one too many female genes or chromosomes. That there was something inherently feminine about him. Late at night in bed he'd poke and jiggle at his stomach and chest and penis, rubbing them, wobbling them, pinching and pulling them and sometimes smacking them, and if finding the results were not what he hoped, would curl over on his side in the dark and wish himself dead. He'd whisper to himself that he was a fatboy. A worthless fat little piece of shit with uneven ears and a weak chin. A slug, Jabba the Hut, Chris Farley, pudgy stodgy useless fat shit.

In his embarrassment of his body and his suspicions of its femininity, Greg had quit the two team sports he'd played, Gaelic football and hurling. As the young men in the changing room had gravitated more and more to taking their dicks out and showing them to each other, Greg had developed a phobia of the benches and showers, always finding a way to arrive either early or late, before ultimately quitting both teams. Without the three times a week fitness sessions, he'd put on even more weight, his clothes getting baggier, his arms less defined.

The upshot was that since leaving the teams, Greg had had a year and a half of all that was different. His growing love of heavy metal came with perks. Hoodies and oversized clothes were not just acceptable but sometimes essential uniform. His hair grew longer to his shoulders and covered his moon face when he wanted it to.

He rejected the goth look, he wasn't a wanker, but he liked his share of Metallica and Motörhead, and they came with loose clothing options. With extra time from missing training, he had free evenings where he could wander and meet other loosely aligned music lovers. He'd become increasingly social, well-liked even, establishing wider connections with rocker types, grungers, some of the goth crowd, a few of the indies. He'd hang with the skaters near the sea sometimes, or the emos huddled around phone speakers in covered car parks. They were mixed-sex groups, and so at mass hangouts in fields after dark, Greg once or twice had been sent into the bushes with another actual person, where he'd kissed and been kissed and had shared the odd fumble. But as his confidence as a person had grown, so too had his shame about his body. The longer he went without showing it, the more an unspoken dread filled him at the prospect of doing so. As he accepted invites to the beach, to cosplay on the green, to go moshing, he produced increasingly transparent or embarrassing reasons to remain clothed: verrucas, eczema, saltwater reactions, fear of sunburn. He knew the day was coming when he would just have to do it, to show his uncovered body to friends and strangers alike. And that was the day he would be pitied and mocked. Sniggered and snickered at, losing all the status he had gained.

Now, his day had come. He'd run out of time, and he was here in this room, with its bunk beds and young men and bodies open and vulnerable. About to not just be seen with his body, but to display it, invite comment on it without any opportunity for retort or rebuttal or escape. He was trapped.

The light rain had let up outside and there were patches of sunlight stretching through the widening gaps of cloud. The room lit briefly, rendering the overhead light useless. Lorcan pressed his weight against the door, ensuring it was locked tight, and called the name.

Greg.

Greg pushed to his feet. The other lads clapped as he pulled the laundry hamper out of his way and scuffed through the floor greasy with hair spray and humidity to the spot in front of the window. He gazed for a moment out the rain-flecked glass to the back field, the long grass buffeting in the wind hammering the Connemara coast. The lads ceased clapping as though sensing the dense cloak of humiliation hanging about his shoulders. Greg turned to face his examiners.

He swayed for a moment on his feet, looking to them, one by one, trying to see some last hint of the respect they had for him that would soon vanish. He dropped his arms down to the end of his t-shirt and pulled half of it up. Where others had been hooted at or wolf-whistled at this point, this time there was instead a nervy silence, like he was a man about to show a terrible, long-hinted-at deformity to a shy new lover. When the t-shirt was half up, he switched his tactic, shoving his elbows inside and pushing it over his head. When he had it off, he pulled it down in front of himself so he could untangle it from his arms, showing his shoulders first as he righted the t-shirt from inside out, getting it ready to put back on quickly. As he fluffed and folded the garment, hiding his chest, he knew he was taking too long, and so inhaled, stood upright, and tossed the t-shirt to the ground.

No one said a word. He felt their eyes scanning him. He pushed his hair back behind his shoulders. He tensed his stomach, tried to make it stand firm and straight, no undulating hills. Then he sucked it in, then he exhaled, letting it go, giving up. Lorcan winced.

Get on with it, Greg said, into the silence.

He closed his eyes as he felt a tug in his lip. He inhaled, and kept his eyes shut. His lips trembled uncontrollably, and even then, he knew he needed to speak.

I know I'm fat, he said. So just get on with it.

You're not fat, dude, came a high-pitched voice from somewhere in the room.

Greg dropped his head and squeezed his eyes shut even tighter, his face warming and throbbing as he tried to keep his head moving to avoid them seeing his lips quivering, his nose leaking.

It's alright, he said. Away you go.

Dude, we're not here to make fun of you.

Go on, he said. Just go on.

He shook his head, opening his eyes but keeping them trained on the ground as they welled up. His vision went blurry and a single hot tear hit the ground by his feet. He stared at its perfect splash mark, then rubbed an open eye with the back of his wrist.

The lads looked to each other, not sure what to do. Lash into him? Let him sit back down? Say forget about it?

Lorcan stepped forward from the door, releasing the handle.

Here, he said. Hold still.

He took a full look, generating an appraisal, as others watched him, Vinny on his side in the bed, his boner gone dormant, Damien leaning back on the wall, Mango by the window and Tetrapak by the radiator. Lorcan tilted his head to the side.

Nah boy, he said. You could lose a little weight, but fat? Far from.

Fuck off, Greg said.

I'm telling you now.

You don't need to bullshit.

I'm not bullshitting you, Lorcan said. C'mere. Stand up straight. Stand up straight, now. Do it.

Greg snuffled his leaking nose and blinked rapidly, trying to smother the tears, then he pulled his head up and his shoulders back.

Lorcan looked at Greg.

You fucking stoop, he said. So you need to stop doing that. It makes you look small, and also it doubles you over and it looks like you're hiding something.

He pursed his lips, then said, Someone else now.

Vinny wiggled forward on the bed.

You do have extra weight on you, he said, letting it sit. But it's not much. Nothing that a month of salad and a few sprints won't solve. Seriously, you'd barely notice it like.

Is that an innie or an outie? Damien asked.

Both, kinda, Greg said, looking.

You've got good shoulders, Lorcan said. Wide fuckers. But you're missing definition on them. Do some push-ups.

Yeah, you look solid like, Mango said. You can tell you have muscles, but they're hardly sculpted or anything.

Him too with the farmer's tan, said Fanning. Get some sun on your body, dude. Stop swimming in your t-shirt.

His left collarbone is higher than his right.

Give us a spin there, Greg.

And Greg did it. He turned. Quickly, but he turned, coming full circle.

He's a big back. You can tell he's strong.

Massive freckles on his shoulders.

And yeah, pull up your jocks like. Or buy a belt. I don't need to see your crack.

So what are we saying, Lorcan said. Defo, get a belt. Work on your shoulders, few sprints.

You need to fix your hair, Sam said from the back.

We're not doing the head this week, Lorcan said. We agreed. But yeah, fix the fringe situation, and use some aftershave or something. Dove For Men isn't cool. Yeah?

He's right, said Fanning.

Stop eating the fucking Maryland biscuits, Vinny said down from his bunk. In a month you'll be the same weight as the rest of us, so don't be giving all this shite about being fat. You're a big lad, and girls like that.

You look good in those check shirts you have, said Mango.

Okay, Lorcan said. Done?

Done, yeah, the lads agreed.

Greg, shirtless, nodded. He bent down, noting the belly rolls that may have folded as he did so, and came up, squeezing the t-shirt into a ball in his hands, still standing there. Not knowing how to return.

Lorcan remained standing in front of Greg. Listen to me, he said. Listen. Are you listening?

Yeah, Greg said.

Are you?

Yeah.

Don't be so down on yourself. It's worse than anything else that's actually fucking wrong with you. Here, you've seen Fitzy, yeah? Blonde Fitzy?

Yeah.

Fucking rotten looking, Lorcan said. The face on him, and the fucked up teeth. But he does unreal with girls. Know why? He's not down on himself.

Greg nodded. He unbunched the t-shirt and pulled it on over his head. He looked around.

Thanks lads, he said.

Then, Lorcan's Barrier failed. The door brushed open, and Lorcan launched himself at it, trying to wedge it back closed.

SKETCH, he said.

Cinnire Paul shoved into the room behind the door using his one free hand, the other occupied texting. Lorcan was flung away by the force of the entry and staggered back against a bunk post. Paul hardly looked up, not caring he'd tossed a fifteen-year-old clear across the room.

Leath an uair, he said, not even glancing up from his screen. *Leathuair agus táimid ag dul.* He turned on the spot and went out again, back to his bunk in the other room, having given his marching orders.

Lorcan closed the door after him, left it a moment, then gave instructions to the rest.

We'll start on the face tomorrow, he said. Or whenever. Now, who has the Paco Rabanne?

And that was that. Shamefully soiled towels were grabbed from the floor, ready for more use. Damien shouted asking did he need a quick shower first, but was ignored by the rest of the lads, who were taking out the good clothes, the shiny black button-downs, the slimfit Calvin Kleins, ironed t-shirts that had been hung delicately from hangers in the closet for the night that would require them. The disco was only an hour away. Phones were taken out, as lads threw cans of deodorant and aftershave to each other about the room. Is double denim acceptable? Are suspenders a good idea? Mango was trialling a fedora and a white tie over a black shirt, Fanning was in the corner scrubbing his Air Jordans with a toothbrush.

In the bathroom, steam took over the windows as Damien showered while the rest wiped the mirror clear of fog and pushed their heads past each other's. Vinny's new hair technique wasn't about product, about L'Oréal Wet Style or Dax Red, but about the method you used to put it in. A little bit placed onto the tips of the fingers and gently fluffed through the hair in a hundred soft plucking motions. He demonstrated on Greg. Tetrapak dabbed some Sauvage by Dior into the palm of his hand, and rubbed it sticky into the skin beneath the waistband of his jeans.

Draws them to the area, he said.

On the half hour Cinnire Paul had promised, he led them from the house, giving Greg a soft boot up the arse as he struggled to loop a belt through the new jeans he'd held in reserve. They made their way from the house, these eight young men and their minder, phones glowing in the fading light. Rain puddles glimmered beside grassy verges as they made their way down the drywalled boreen, past fields and trees, the sky a drained yellow before the gloaming, bigging

each other up and tapping messages, laying
foundations for later, saying Sylvia's messaged me
back, sent me a selfie. Tigh Neachtain posted on
Instagram, they're unreal looking. Rides. Cinnire
Paul with his head down, pretending not to hear
the béarlachas, himself messaging Val his new
girlfriend, he'd meet her at the gate with her
seven young women, dump their charges at the
disco and head off somewhere quiet themselves.
Greg, thick among the group, his shiny navy
shirt stretched tight across his shoulders, his new
jeans on, with friends, felt good, part of something.
The Lynx-soaked stink of hair wax and suncream
on cotton was about them, a catastrophe of
scents shuffling towards the school gates for the
black night of close contact in hidden corners,
while teachers of Irish stood back by the doors
promising to have a drink later once the young
ones had had their fill of each other, which
they'd have already set to doing, combining and
separating and pulling close again, cherry gloss
lips slicking against sun-chapped mouths,
shoulders smacked well done by palms, caught
breaths and selfies and sneakings of vodka passed
and heat and sweat and tenderness in a long dark
room with shoe-scraped floors, body pressed
against body.

Night Train

Georgina Harding

THE RAILWAY STATION IS crowded and dark like wartime. There was the high grand entrance where the taxi had dropped her, all but blacked out so that she had stumbled on the steps, and now soaring Art Nouveau waiting halls with low ranks of benches where shadowy people sit bundled up in the cold, because there is as little heating as there is light, and the nights are cold now. She has got there early, like them, and waited and frozen awhile and studied the names on the departure board before going to her platform, and still there are some fifteen minutes before the train is due. If when it finally comes it turns out to be a steam engine, this will not surprise her. She imagines the whistle, the sound of it, smoke billowing beneath the high glass roof, a scramble of passengers like refugees with pale glimpsed faces. In reality, it is all quite modern and orderly, a noticeboard on the platform where you can find the position of your numbered sleeper – or at least you can if you use the light of your phone – the train dead on time, a neat conductor stepping out to check your reservation as you board, the carriage itself clean and spacious. It is just an oddity of this country that all the long-distance trains travel at night. And that the stations are dim.

She is in Lvov which used to be called Lviv and was once called Lemburg, and she is taking the night train to Kiev, in Ukraine but it used to be Russia to her, the USSR, and really, aside from the names, she knows almost nothing about these places. Take a trip, her friends said, it'll be good for you, this year of all years. Of course, they likely meant the south of France or Italy, somewhere with a chance of sunshine in November, and good food and art to see. But this trip just fitted itself together. Stephen had wanted to celebrate his sixtieth with a weekend break in Krakow where his grandmother had been born and where he had never been, and she had happened to read a book about Lvov in the war, and she has a married niece whose husband has been posted to Kiev. It was her niece, knowing this part of the world, who had the idea that she should make the intervening journeys by train.

Have fun, Stephen said before he flew home from Krakow, and, roll on retirement then he'd travel too. Only she didn't believe him, as she never quite believed his talk of winters they would spend in Italy when the tourists weren't there.

'You don't mean that. You'd hate being retired.'

'You're probably right,' he said. 'You travel. I'll stay home. So long as you come back.'

'Of course I'll come back. Soon.'

At the last minute, another woman enters the compartment. Pity. She thought she might have it to herself. *Over-coloured*, she thinks. This woman is a whirl of colour after all that drab. Red hair that must be grey underneath, hat like a tea cosy, lime-green rucksack, large pink suitcase, cheeks flushed from running. She retracts into her Englishness as the train departs. Perhaps that shows, her Englishness. Or there is the *Barchester Towers* on her lap. Trollope is more Stephen's thing than her own, but she had happened to find it in the English-language bookshop in Krakow after he left and thought she would read it for company.

Likely it was the Trollope that gave her away. The woman is an English teacher, Alice will discover, as Alice's mother had been.

'Hello.'

'Hello.'

'Tourist?'

'Yes, tourist.'

The journey looks routine to her. Possibly the hurry too, so habitually chaotic she looks. She takes a few things out of the rucksack and then hoists it onto the rack opposite Alice's. The case is patently too heavy for that. It stands like a boulder in the space between the seats. Very pink. Scuffed with use. Right now, Alice resents it. Later, as the train runs on into the dark and the night passes and she sleeps and wakes, and lies awake perhaps more than she sleeps, she will be glad of the woman's presence, as if she herself emanates some colour. As if the darkness would be too black if she were not there. Or indeed, the case.

The train moves and slows and halts, runs on for stretches as it seems infinitesimally slowly and then rushes ahead awhile, stops again at stations where the light comes bright around the edges of the window blind, and Alice peeks out to try to see the name of the place and there is only brightness and the bare platform and nobody there, until at some junction there is movement and clatter in the empty space, and the carriage jolts as the train is divided or another train is added on to it.

'Where are we?' The voice says from the other bunk.

'I don't know, I couldn't see.'

The voice names some station halfway. Maybe that's where they are. Alice has never heard of the place.

'Have you been to this country before?'

'No. This is the first time.'

They get talking then, in the dark. There aren't many tourists nowadays, the woman says. In fact, there never have been many tourists. A lot of foreigners don't even seem to know they are a country, a proper country and not a part of Russia. Does she understand that? Yes, she says. At least, she knows it now, being here. Before she came, she had thought it was all wheatfields. And tractors, and big smiling farm girls like in the propaganda, the voice says. Yes, she says. She likes this woman's voice. It has a laugh in it. They are still at whatever station it is. The train has been stationary for a long time. She pulls at the blind again and looks out at the bare platform. Why do you look, there's nothing to see? No, there's nothing to see. They fall silent and after what seems a long time more the train, at last, gives a slow sigh and begins to move.

'What is your name?'

'Alice.' She thought the woman was asleep but she isn't.

'Iryna.'

The train is gathering speed.

'Goodnight Alice.'

'Goodnight.'

The night train doesn't have to hurry, she thinks. Its schedule is designed to fill time as much to reach the destination. To fill the night so that it is morning when they arrive. A journey can be any length. And sometimes a night itself can seem immeasurable. She listens to the rhythm of the train on the tracks and her companion's gentle snoring.

She lies awake too long. Sometimes in the small hours, she needs to use the toilet. She thinks about it a long time before she tells herself she really has to go. She wraps herself in her coat, feels around for shoes, and when finally she finds them she opens the door of the compartment, starts out into the brightness of the corridor, steps back quickly as she sees a figure at the end of the carriage. It is only a man who has used the toilet before her, a fat man in a vest groping his way into a far compartment. She doesn't know if he's aware of her, hanging back as she does in her own doorway.

She closes the door as quietly as she can so as not to wake her fellow traveller and goes lightly up the corridor, putting her hand out to the walls and the windows to steady herself, half-asleep as she is, against the jolting of the train. At one moment she finds herself almost thrown against the glass. And her reflection flashes there, ghostly, monochrome, old – older than she thinks she is, with her hair mussed about her head, the hair grey, entirely grey, no sign left of its carefully tended blondeness.

She is suddenly afraid, so fragile she looks. Immaterial. There was a film, wasn't there, where a woman disappeared from a train? She has the sound of it about her, the rattle of the train on the tracks, rushing through blackness. An elderly woman disappeared from a train, but before she disappeared, she drew with her finger the clue to some mystery in the condensation on the window, words that were suddenly revealed when the train went through a tunnel. Was the old woman a spy? Where was she travelling? The Alps, perhaps. Germany, Austria, Switzerland, somewhere like that, somewhere with mountains, not flat like this. And a younger Englishwoman, some crisply spoken, well made-up fellow passenger, gets somehow drawn into the plot. She can't remember anything else about the film just then.

The Lady Vanishes. That's it. Back in her bunk she listens to the train and remembers the name of the film. Hitchcock. Black-and-white. Early Hitchcock, it must have been, before he went to Hollywood.

The old lady vanished. Miss Foy, that was her name. The younger woman keeps asking, 'Where is Miss Foy?'

She thought of her mother. Her mother had loved that film, could have told you the name of every main character and the actors who played them. Even at the end, she might have remembered that.

Her mother had vanished not in any single instant but slowly over time.

The woman in the bunk opposite turns over, moves about. Alice wonders if she too is awake. Iryna. And she is Alice. 'Alice,' a nice woman once said, 'That's a pretty name.' And gave her a two-shilling piece. It was one of those childhood memories that stayed with her. How this nice woman, a neighbour she must have been, someone from the village who knew about them and knew that her father had left them, took pity on her and gave her two shillings. And she had thought, Alice, that's me, that's who the woman is seeing, and I have two shillings in my hand. Alice was a skinny little thing with curls of blonde hair. That was who she was. There are moments when identity crystallises and you know precisely who you are which may perhaps coincide with how you appear in the world outside. That might be why she has kept the memory, because in that moment, she was sure. There are other moments when identity dissolves. Those there is little reason to remember. There are so many such moments, day to day, in which she might not be Alice at all.

The train is running smoothly now. They must be covering ground, the train cutting through the night, covering the miles, passing through unseen unknown land, villages, a town with a lit station where it doesn't stop. Passing a train coming the other way, a shudder as the two streams of air collide. A goods train, it must have been, by the long clanking that followed and ran on like an echo. One of those long European trains that travel a whole continent. There is something comforting in that, in the thought of the length of it, the innumerable wagons travelling innumerable miles, wagon upon wagon, like the sheep you were supposed to count to send you to sleep; and thinking that she does sleep a bit. Then sometime later she is awake again and knows that the other woman also is awake, moving around, unsure whether it is the woman's movement that has woken her or whether she had awoken already. The woman is finding her slippers and unlocking the door as she had earlier, and going out, leaving the door open a crack so the light of the corridor seeps in. Alice reaches out and pulls the door to and lies awake in the dark listening, alert like prey, knowing that for these few minutes anyone might enter, until the woman returns, unseen but heard, as she locks it once more and shuffles back into her bed and spends some time rearranging herself in the sheets. Should they speak? No, not now, not until daylight.

There had been nights in her mother's house waiting for light. She had taken time off from work to look after her through those last weeks, sleeping in an adjoining room but with the doors open so that she could hear her movement and sometimes her breathing, lying awake then and listening when her sleep was disturbed and when she was silent as if she might already have died. Then her senses reached out through the darkness to feel if she was still alive, but she had to wait until daylight to be sure. And when the first light came, if she had not fallen asleep herself, she would creep to the door and see the old woman lightly breathing as the birdsong came through the open window but muted because these were mornings of high summer and even the birds were lazy. They seemed like a dream now, those days. They were outside all of the rest of life. When

Stephen or one of the girls came at weekends, or all of them at the very end making the journey down to Sussex, she had felt detached even from them.

The train has slowed again. It has crept along for a while and then halted altogether. They are nowhere and she wonders why she has come.

She had wanted her mother not to go. The days were beautiful. The sunlight played its way across the bedroom as the days passed, lighting the pictures, the mirror, the lamps, the motes in the air. Sometimes she had to draw the curtains when the light fell directly onto the bed. She drew the shadow across her mother's face and her hands on the sheet. Her eyes were closed in those days more than they were open. She wanted them open. She wanted them to see. She wanted to see even a shimmer of them between the lids.

The others floated in and out of the room. Go outside, they said to her. We'll sit. You go out and take some air. How could she say that she couldn't bear to, that she was only herself as long as she remained? And yet she did go out, and they were right. It was good to be out. And really it made no difference to her mother by then which one of them was there.

Everyone would say later that the timing was in its way a relief, before the dementia entirely took her, when there were still moments when she was herself. And how good that they could all be there, and that the summer was so lovely outside. Those last few days were like a house party, with one or other of the girls baking cakes and opening photograph albums and memories.

Stay, she said to her mother in the night. Just stay. Stay here. Stay with me. Reaching out to her in the darkness.

And now she is travelling alone. The threads are cut. She has cut loose, for the first time in her life. She is on a train passing through places whose names she cannot read, let alone pronounce. Look, Mum. Open your eyes just a little bit wider and look where I am now. On a train in the night, going east. Like in one of those old films you used to watch.

Like the films they saw on their rare nights out, to the Essoldo in town. The first film she saw in a cinema was *Swiss Family Robinson* (little thinking that she herself would end up a Robinson, marrying a man whose family had once come out of that east where she now is and taken that name in place of some other name in the new country to which they had come). But as soon as she was old enough her mother began to take her to the sort of grown-up films she liked to watch, evening showings not matinées, she her mother's companion as well as her daughter. In those days, when the film was over, you all stood as the credits rolled and remained standing afterwards as the national anthem played before you filed out into the street, and just at that moment, as they came out, her mother would light a cigarette, and Alice would know by the way she smoked it that part of her was still in the film. She could look beautiful, her mother, when she carried herself that particular way. She had those lovely blue eyes, and blonde hair and a pretty figure, and could have made more of herself if she had tried. But why try when you stood in front of a class of twenty girls all day in a convent school in a small Sussex town? When you stood at a blackboard with chalk on your fingers teaching them grammar. Those were the days when children were still taught subjects and predicates, dividing sentences up into their parts, forming them according to absolute rules. That wasn't a job for a woman who looked like a film star, or even a starlet, which was all her mother might have hoped to be, beautiful as she was or could be but not in any special way, shapely in the style of the day, pouting just so little as she let the smoke go from her lips. What her mother really wanted to do was teach the children to imagine and to feel. To give them literature.

Make them know other lives. Put stories in their heads.

The chalk got everywhere. When she cleaned the board with the rubber the wiped dust settled in her clothes. When she came home, she smelled of chalk. Even when she had changed it was there in her hair.

Her mother would like to have done what she was doing now. To travel on a train through Eastern Europe in the night, feeling the alien ground pass beneath her, heading towards an unknown city. Her mother had expressed appropriate pride to see her daughter become a lawyer, in the man's world that it was then, and marry a nice man too, one who was warm and amusing and yet steady. Only she had formed a habit from early on of speaking of him as 'your Stephen,' as if he were a sought-after commodity but only one of a number such that might be found. Alice felt that she was also faintly disappointed that she had effectively chosen the grammar over the literature. But look, Mum. Look at me now. So often a child will say that, so often her own children had said that, making a painting, swinging terrifyingly high on a swing, learning to dive, diving into a pool. Look where I am. Deep behind the Iron Curtain. I know, it's not there anymore, it hasn't been there already for decades, but the language and the towns and the landscape are the same. And the train runs on the same lines, those wide Russian tracks that were meant to stop invading armies, and there's a samovar at the end of the carriage and in the morning the conductor will pour hot water from it onto tea in a glass set into a metal holder.

She has slept at last, though she had come to think that she wouldn't. She has slept through the gloaming and the dawn, and when she opens her eyes, the light is already bright behind the blind. The other woman has opened it just a little and is looking out.

'It's alright, I'm awake, you can open it now.'

She takes her wash things with her and a water bottle, and goes to the cramped toilet and washes minimally and cleans her teeth, and tries to do something with her hair. When she gets back there is the conductor's tea, and Iryna shares with her some buns that she had brought with her for breakfast. Alice has brought nothing, expecting there to be a restaurant car. They sit by the window and rest their glasses on the little shelf beneath it and look out, Alice looking ahead to where they are going, the woman looking back to where they have been. There is still an hour or more to go before they reach the city. The landscape is disappointingly similar to the one they left, or what Alice had seen when she entered the country, low-lying forest and patches of farmland, long villages, dreary towns, roads where cars take people to work, a few cows, a solitary tractor.

'No wheatfields.'

'No. Though I suppose some of these fields are wheat in the summer.'

'Not what you expected.'

'Yes. No. I don't know what I expected.' She might have told her that it is only on a whim that she came at all.

'How long will you be here?'

'I fly back next week. I'm staying with my niece.'

'A week, that's good. You need a week to get some sense of the place. Not only to see the sights.'

The woman tells her what the sights are that she should see, the restored churches and the ancient monastery with its underground complex of caves – that at least the Soviets had not destroyed – the ravine where there had been a terrible massacre in thewar, the Maidan where the recent revolution took place.

'I can show you that,' she says. 'I was there.'

Alice vaguely remembers reading it in the papers. She seems to remember that people were killed on the Maidan, or perhaps that was some other revolution. She has never paid these things enough attention.

'I would be happy to show you around one day, perhaps one afternoon after school, if you would like that. I finish early some afternoons.'

'That's very kind,' Alice says. Though she is sure that her niece will have plans.

See, Mum. This woman is my age. She has grown up under Communism and seen a revolution – or two revolutions – wasn't there an Orange one as well? – or maybe three, however many revolutions it is that they've had here. She's the sort of person you'd want to meet. She speaks of the revolution, of whichever revolution it was, with the bright sad kind of look in her eyes with which one might recall a past lover. Do you think it's like that, revolutions like passionate love affairs, ending in nostalgia or maybe bitterness, that that's how it is? She would like the conversation to carry further but the train has slowed again, to a snail's pace, and words slow with it. Such a long train, she can see that looking ahead as they so slowly curve about a bend, see the carriages ahead of her as Iryna can see the carriages behind. Her voice fades, silence falls, each woman falling into her thoughts until the train regathers speed. Two women at a picture window, a worn strip of flowered carpet on the floor between the seats like a notion of home, and the framed trees begin to pass quickly now, grey bark, white bark, fallen, falling leaves, pines dull green, more pines, more birches, tree after tree in the thin early light.

This time of the morning in her mother's house. No, not this time. This is November. It was in April, May, that she had gone to her mother's house, when her mother could still get around, just about. Late spring, early summer, but some equivalent time after dawn when the day will be fine and the sunlight is crisp and low, and she wakes early, looking out of a window and seeing her mother. She is walking in her nightdress, in her thin cotton dressing gown, the dressing gown open like a cloak and her hands in its pockets, out into the orchard where the apples are in blossom, standing and staring in the long grass and the cowslips. Alice runs down, brings her mother in. 'There's so much to see', her mother says. Her slippers and the hem of her nightdress are soaked with dew.

They are coming to the city edges. They would, if the train had not stopped just then, have only another fifteen or at most twenty minutes before they reach the station, after which they need never see one another again. It suddenly makes it easy to talk, looking out ahead and behind along the line.

'You're a teacher, you say?'

'Yes, I teach English.'

'My mother was an English teacher. I studied it at university. Later I thought I should have studied History instead.'

'Why is that?'

'Because history has a purpose. What you are studying really happened.'

'But stories can tell us real things,' she says. And then she adds, 'Sometimes they say more than events.'

They talk on. They tell each other who they are. Alice says that she is a lawyer and a mother of three. She has a husband, daughters, no sons. She realises as she speaks that she might tell this stranger anything, here on this train. She might say she is a businesswoman, a pianist, a spy. She could tell her a fiction and it could seem just as true.

Iryna has one son.

Iryna is divorced. Alice has thought she seems too individual to live with a partner, except a female one perhaps.

Iryna comes from the east of the country where there is a war going on. Her parents are still there. She has told them they could come and live with her in the city but they insist on staying where they are, where they have a vegetable patch and fruit trees and a cow. How could they live with her and her son in a two-bedroom fifth-floor flat with a balcony no bigger than a sofa? Alice sees that they have a point, even if there is a war going on.

I'm travelling because my mother died, Alice says. It's OK, she says, cutting short an expression of condolence, her mother had been very frail for a long time, it had been very much expected, the timing in fact almost a mercy. But it took a while to adjust to these things. To get back to being who you were.

Then travelling must be a good thing for her to do, Iryna says. She travels a lot herself. She travels all over the place, and whenever possible by train. You meet so many people when you travel, it's good for you, she says, and you find stories because every day can be different from the one before. And grief needs stories, doesn't it?

Perhaps it is because of grief, because of death, that people made up stories in the first place, when facts, history, material explanations, just weren't enough. Her country, for example, is full of stories. It has to be because it has experienced so much grief.

I have no story, Alice thinks. *Only a life that runs day to day. No history behind me, no revolution, no war. None of this woman's vividness.*

'You should keep a diary,' Iryna says. 'Of your travels.'

If she had a diary, what would she write?

Iryna is tidying her bedding away, the green rucksack brought down, her night things packed away into it, the rucksack and the pink suitcase crowding her out on the seat, the tea cosy hat beside her, her coat hanging from the hook. Alice has kept whatever was needed for the night separate in her white canvas bag, and her suitcase had remained locked on the rack all the journey. She had been pleased when she had packed that she had kept her luggage so neat, precisely arranged, easily manageable. She had prided herself that for this trip she would be travelling light. Shall I help you take it down, Iryna had asked, and she had said, no, no, thank you, that's fine, I can do it when we get there. Only they haven't got there yet. They are stopped once again at some place where a dozen rusted railway lines converge. They have the compartment door open now and can see, through the windows on both sides, line after line of tracks, and beyond the tracks, wastelands of scrapyards and warehouses and apartment blocks and graffitied walls, the concrete fringe of city – of any city, Alice tells herself, even the beautiful cities begin like this. In truth, she is a little afraid of Kiev.

The train is late.

The conductor comes down the corridor and explains the delay. A signal failure. They hope to be moving soon. Once again there is tea in a glass in a metal holder. The train is so still that she can hear the other woman sip.

They should have arrived by now. If the train had arrived on time, they would have bustled out onto the station minutes ago and already have said goodbye.

The delay is unusual, Iryna says. She does this journey regularly and this is the first time the train has come in late. Punctuality, she says, is one of the better Soviet legacies.

Oh really, says Alice, good for you. In her experience as often as not you expect a journey to contain pauses like this, moments of emptiness. All those journeys she had made to visit her mother in Sussex, taking the train as often as not because she so hated the drive, fitting the journey in when she could with meetings in London. Ah, Alice, so you're here at last, her mother would say, though she was actually quite unaware of the time and would have said the same if she had been early. At least on those train journeys, she could get some work done. Now in the silence, she takes up her *Barchester Towers* and tries to remember where she has got to.

The train moves a little way then stops again. She looks out at the tracks which are the same tracks she has looked out at earlier, only a little further along. The purple graffiti she has glimpsed from a distance on a stretch of concrete wall beside the tracks is right in front of them now, in roman script but even so, she can't make sense of it. It looks angry like graffiti everywhere. She returns to her book and finds herself back at the beginning of a paragraph she has read earlier. She closes the book and looks up and out of the window once more.

She has to go to the toilet again. They have drunk too much tea. The toilet has grown more sordid as the morning has progressed, seat up and untouchable, bin overflowing with paper. She washes her hands quickly, catching brief sight of herself in the stained mirror.

A private moment. Her mother in a private moment, looking into the bathroom mirror in one of those private moments that are no longer private when a person is so lost and feeble that they have to be helped to the bathroom, that someone else must be there to help them pee. She had helped her mother to the room, to pee, wipe, stand before the basin and the mirror, and her mother took from the shelf there a brush to brush her hair in the mirror. Her hand quivered with each feeble stroke, her hair so fine that brushing it was only token movement. The skin on her hand and face seemed insubstantial against the hardness of the glass and the reflected turquoise of the tiles on the wall behind her.

When she was done, her hand hovered for an instant before it placed the brush back on the shelf beside the tooth mug and the bottles. She leant forward and looked into her face as if it was new to her, eyes to eyes in the glass narrowing with some thought. And spoke in a firm voice, firm and hopeful, 'I want a real life.'

As if it was a normal thing to demand. A cup of tea. An apple. A real life. She heard that her mother spoke in the present tense, not the past.

'What's that, Mum?' She put a hand soft to the old woman's shoulder to shepherd her away from the mirror and out of the hard tight too-bright room.

'You know, dear, a real life.' (Why is it her mother, women of her age, would only say 'dear' when they were cross?) 'Like in stories. Like other people have, those people you read about.'

'What do you mean, Mum?'

'A great love. An adventure. A career. A life,

that's what I want. Something happening. Something like that.' That was all. Her chin raised in the mirror image as she turned away, three-quarter view, like a teenager experimenting with an adult look.

If the train had not been stopped so long, if there had not been that emptiness, Iryna would not have opened her case.

'Look, shall I show you what I have?'

A show-woman's case. A case of colour. The battered pink case unzips to reveal a zebra-skin lining and a riot of crochet-work folded and wrapped in tissue. Colour showing through to colour, pink to green to purple. Iryna removes the tissue layer by layer, pulls out a shawl and then a quilt, spreads them across the narrow seats.

'I get them from the villages. The women make them to raise money for the war.' Quilts, shawls, blankets, throws, so many colours unfolding.

'Perhaps you would like to buy one?'

Scarlet, yellow, indigo, lilac. Rainbows of colour.

'At the beginning, our soldiers didn't even have boots. Now we are getting them night-vision optics.'

Alice doesn't know what she'll do with it but she picks out something in a relatively tasteful range of ochres.

(That's a bit bright, isn't it, Stephen will say when she unpacks. What are you going to do with that? She will think, well yes, it does look rather bright now she has it home. She had told herself it might be considered autumnal but really it's garish. It's for the war, she will say. She couldn't help but buy it. So that snipers can see in the dark. And Stephen will laugh, well they'll certainly be able to see that.)

Iryna puts the money into her wallet then reaches into a corner of the case. 'Please, take this. I'd like to give you this.'

A pot of honey.

Her mother's honey from Donbas. Every couple of months she makes this journey, carrying pots of her mother's honey to sell in a market in Lvov alongside wooden handicrafts and Putin-printed toilet roll, bringing back to Kiev quilts to sell for weaponry.

'Your mother keeps bees?'

'Bees don't mind about the war.'

An old woman in Donbas puts on her beekeeper's veil, goes to tend her bees. Walks through the grass beneath the apple trees where a path winds through to the hives. There are soldiers on the road in front of the house. There may be a sound of gunfire across the fields. The old woman looks out through the veil. She has eyes, ears, only for the bees. She removes a tray from the hive and the bees form a cloud around her until she can no longer be seen.

🐾 Toadstone

Danny Rhodes

Up through the terraced streets, then along the wide avenue lined with bigger houses until he reaches the 1930s Art Deco hospital, where he crosses the busy car park, follows the arrow down a little conduit to a sliding door.

Out of place here. Viewed strangely. But perhaps that's just in his head. The nurse is friendly enough, the young trainee nurse (Is it okay if she observes?), shy and embarrassed. He holds his stomach in, smiles (Sure).

'I'll guide you in,' says the nurse. 'Ooh, not in a rude way.'

Like a Carry On film. Sid James. Barbara Windsor. You have to laugh.

Then the machine (cold and angular) that compresses his breast tissue, squeezes it flat while he stands staring at the bare walls.

'It might be uncomfortable,' says the nurse

from behind the screen. 'It might be painful.' And it is.

But then it's done. It's over. He's getting dressed.

'…within two weeks,' she says.

'Two weeks,' he says.

'…if there's anything sinister.'

Sinister.

But he's here now, doing something about it. So there's that to be said, and he says it, smiles, pulls on his shirt, nods to the trainee (who smiles in return) as he makes his way out. The waiting room is full of women. One looks at him as he leaves, looks puzzled, is wondering, no doubt, what he's doing there. Then he's away from the place.

He makes his way home. Glad it's over. Or beginning. Just have to wait and see. Best not tell anybody. Best not share.

Probably nothing. Almost certainly nothing. So why mention it? Why tell? Certainly not his parents who have enough on their plate already. Certainly not his mother.

'Rob and Judy,' she says. 'Josie and Dave. Lots of people you don't know. We're getting too old for it really. But then you think of the toads.'

'Okay, Mum,' he says. 'I can come for a few days.'

'That's lovely,' she says. 'I'll let Derek know.'

He puts the phone down, wanders into the living room. One of the cats has requisitioned the sofa. It opens an eye, stretches, looks at him, and then closes it again. He fetches the box of photographs from upstairs and places it on the dining room table, continues the job he committed to several weeks before.

The photographs stretch back over 60 years. Tiny black-and-white photographs of his father and mother when they first met. Images of them as a newly married couple. Young. Trendy. The new estate. Uniform gardens. Uniform lives. Him as a small child in preposterous clothes. His grandparents in their garden amongst their roses. His grandfather's suit. His grandmother's frock. The photographs changing, becoming colour, larger, richer. Family holidays. Seasides and seascapes. His bleach blonde brother. Past Christmases too. Year upon year. Everybody together. Because that's how it was. Fashions shifting. Hairstyles. Vehicles. Pets. School uniforms. First days. His brother the sports captain. His brother's graduation. His brother's wedding. His parents in their fifties. In their sixties. In their seventies.

The last batch. Numerous sets of his parents with their friends. Not so long ago. Not really. A decade perhaps. All the friends together. On a day trip somewhere. On one of their adventures. Beryl eating an ice cream on a harbour wall. Dave leading the way up some remote country path. Pictures of them laughing. Having fun. The whole crowd. Jon in his wheelchair, the life and soul. Pat laughing along with him. The camera invading a moment, capturing it, burying it in time. Some sort of embarrassing event. Hysterics all round. Judy and Rob. Ken and Sue. Eating. Drinking. Falling over. More laughter. Everybody laughing. And then the decline. The little gang diminishing. He sifts through, sorting years from years, separating the living from the dead. Individuals conspicuous by their absence.

Cancer. Heart disease. You know how it is.

He can't say 'no' to his mother's latest request. He can't do that. His parents' world is shrinking around them. It's the least he can do. And it will be good to go back, he supposes. Good to return from whence he came.

It's raining when he leaves the city and it rains for the whole of his journey north, the landscape shifting as he travels, becoming flatter, emptier, the darkness expanding all around him. He's found an annexe for rent in the village where his grandparents lived. A stone's throw from the church. One bedroom. A tiny kitchen. Cosy though. Welcoming. The owners are new to the area, commuter types. There are advantages if you can stand the hours by train (they say). If you can stomach the claustrophobia of village life (they say).

If.

He wakes early on the first morning. It's brighter, unseasonably warm, though he can still smell the rain and he appreciates the scent of it, the freshness it delivers. He wanders, instinctively, down the back lane past the village school in the direction of the churchyard. Little has changed. The church set on a mound. The graves high above the lane. The bowing stone wall holding everything back. The extended cemetery continues on the other side of the lane. He enters through the rusting iron gates connecting the two, skirts its edge until he reaches his grandparents' gravestone. A book design. Two adjacent pages. Their names side by side.

Reunited.

He places some pebbles on the headstone (that needs a clean), embarrassed he's brought nothing with him, hasn't thought things through. And then he stands there for a time, the morning sun on his face. He closes his eyes.

Melancholy's the word. Or perhaps it isn't. Not *melas* (black), not *kholé* (bile). Wistful then.

Wistful's more accurate. How he feels today. Hardly surprising. Being here. Being where he once was.

He retreats, considers his next move, thinks of the little sweet shop his grandmother would walk him to on their way back from the grocery store. Just a house now. But once it was Raymond's. The ringing of the bell. The darkness within. Raymond in his brown jacket. The jars of sweets. The scoop. The weighing scales. White mice in a brown paper bag. The old ladies of the village cooing over him as they make their way back up the steep hill. Pats on the head. The sound of the radio in his grandmother's kitchen. His grandmother busy there. The smell of baking. Always that smell. And his grandmother's cigarettes. The coal fire. The tick-tock of the grandfather clock, marking the seconds, marking the minutes, marking the hours. The summers and the winters of his childhood.

He circles the village with these things in mind. Just to feel. Just to see what might emerge from all of this.

And there are echoes everywhere. The willow tree and the water feature his grandfather signed off during his time on the village council. The war memorial. The family name. Great Grandfather John. Ypres. 1917. That doesn't bear thinking about, though perhaps he should. The little cottage where his father was born. The old pub at the top of the hill, a set of separate dwellings now, gone forever. The bungalow where his grandparents retired.

FOR SALE.

Well there's a turn up. There's a surprise. It looks empty too. He stands at the gate and stares. Stands and stares.

He takes out his phone. He dials the agent's number. 'Tomorrow,' suggests the agent.

'Yes,' he says. 'Yes.'

He follows the boundary to the back of the property, stands by the stone wall overlooking the garden, recalls the winter of heavy snowfall, the deep drifts of snow, the muffled January stillness. An owl had flown across the field. He remembers how the owl frightened him, its ghost-white wings, its soundless flight. He stands there for a time, lost in thought. Then he moves on to the old quarry. New houses there now. A new lane. But there's a gap in the wire fencing, a way in. He pushes through it, sidles down the steep slope, reaches the quarry floor. So much smaller to him now. So much shallower than he remembers. And so much lost. But so much remains if you care to look. The same scrubby plants, the same exposed rock. He drops to his haunches, scrabbles around, unearths a hunk of limestone, picks it up, turns it over in his palms, unearths and turns over other things too. Innumerable memories. Fossil hunting with the boys of the village. Hot summer days. The sun on the yellow stone. The dryness and the dust. On his clothes. On his bare knees. In his hair.

He puts the stone back. He took one from the quarry on the day his grandfather died but it crumbled in the first frost, unable to survive its relocation. And he wonders why that is, what factors allow for something to endure in one place and yet succumb in another. He tentatively presses two fingers against his breast, thinks of the nurse in the little room, the sound of her voice.

Sinister.

But hey-ho. No news is good news. He clambers out of the quarry, crosses the lane to a gateway opposite, hops over it, follows the track up the incline towards the pond. As his father did. As his grandfather did. As his father did before him. As *he* did as a child. He can feel something, a recoupling, barely perceptible remembrances linking together, fragile to the touch. He spots the line of the Roman road, recalls walks on a Sunday afternoon. Family walks. Everyone together. Conker collecting in the Autumn.

Further off, the windmill stump, a brown protuberance in the flat landscape, a structure that still bears the family name. But only if you know. Only if you care to know. And he wonders how much longer it will remain, how much life it has left and what will happen when it crumbles to nothing and is lost.

They collected the conkers in plastic bags, stored them in the garage until they turned white with mould. Funny what you remember. Funny what you forget.

The path ahead of him narrows. He reaches a cluster of trees, ducks under briar stems and squeezes through ever-smaller gaps between the branches. And for a moment he's a boy again, ten years old, his fishing basket strapped to his back, the scent of spring in his nostrils, green fronds and tender shoots. The same feeling in the base of his spine.

Anticipation. Excitement. The clear bank ahead. The blue water. The newly dredged pond ripe for a boy and his grandfather to fish in. For a second he feels the searing regret at never having children and the gnawing realisation that perhaps he never will and then he catches the scent of stagnant water, notices the overgrown bank, the unchecked, strangling weed, and he comes upon the catastrophe of what is before him.

In the afternoon he drives to his parents' place in the nearby town, the house where he grew up. More memories here of course, but memories he's processed time and time ago. His mother makes him lunch. Mashed potatoes. Mince and onion. He sits with her in the little kitchen, staring out into the garden.

'Your dad's at the hospital,' she says.

'How is dad?' he asks.

'As well as can be expected,' she says.

'Good,' he says. He stuffs some mashed potato into his mouth.

'I've been sorting your photographs,' he says.

'Photographs?'

'The photographs you asked me to go through. The photographs you asked me to sort.'

'Oh,' says his mother. 'Oh.'

He visits the bathroom, opens the cabinet and looks at the many boxes of pills. He remembers a time when there was only his father's razors and shaving foam, a box of aspirin, some plasters. He thinks about his own cabinet and what it contains and what it might contain a few months from now if his life takes a certain direction.

He closes the cabinet and looks at himself in the mirror, splashes his face with water, blows out his cheeks. He is older. Of course he is. And what would his father say if this dark thing were to happen? What would he say? That it's better than the alternative. That things are always better than the alternative.

Downstairs, he stops in the living room, looks at the photographs on the mantelpiece, newly taken photographs of his brother, his brother's wife, their three children. In the corner, he locates a lone photograph of himself from years before, barely recognises the person staring back at him.

'Derek wants us there at seven,' his mother says when he returns to the kitchen. 'To get us up to speed. So we'll –'

'I'll meet you in the lane,' he says. 'I know where it is.'

The lane connects the village to its neighbouring village. A locals lane. Or a cut through from the A road for those with local knowledge. Hence the need for a Toading Group. Hence his parents volunteering each Spring.

The old crossing cottage. The abandoned branch line. A half-healed wound in the landscape. He meets them as planned, meets Derek, meets Derek's wife Julie, meets the rest. All sorts. All ages. Something of a surprise really. One called Dawn. Of a similar age to himself.

His father is there. You wouldn't know, he thinks. You wouldn't guess.

'Evening Son,' says his father, and nods.

'Evening Dad,' he says.

'The pond's up there,' says Derek, addressing the new people. 'That's where they return each Spring. That's where they were born.'

He points across the lane and into the trees.

'The majority of them hibernate down there,' he says. 'In the bottom wood.'

He's never set foot in there. It's too damp, too dark.

Full of mystery. As boys, they were afraid of the place.

'Round about now,' says Derek, 'when the temperature hits a number, when there's a good moon, they make their way up the rise to the pond. To get there they have to cross the lane.

And that's where we come in.'

He thinks about the job of getting something there safely, wonders if he might have been good at that, built for it even. A daughter perhaps. Guiding her through the labyrinth. But nothing has come to him.

'They're awkward creatures. Clumsy. Rather slow,' says Derek (gesturing). 'And some of them like to daydream when they reach the asphalt. It's like something comes over them. They just sit there in harm's way. Then a car comes along and, well, you can imagine. So you've got your signs and your reflective jackets and your torches and your surgical gloves and for the next few nights, we'll station ourselves along this stretch and try to stop such tragedies from happening. Most of the drivers will stop and wait and some of them will get out and give you a hand but some are just bastards.'

The regulars nod their heads. He sees his mother and father nodding and a quiet murmur runs amongst them.

'Bastards.'

'Dawn,' says Derek. 'If you could take this chap (pointing) with you and focus on the section where the track crosses the lane. Or where the lane crosses the track. Be careful though. It gets boggy down there.'

The regulars laugh. The short straw then. Or a test. Or something. He follows after Dawn, catches up with her.

'Here we are then,' she says.

'Yes,' he says. 'Here we are.'

'Your first time?' asks Dawn.

'Yes,' he says.

'My second season,' she says. 'Last year I was an apprentice, now they've given me one.'

Not much happens. It has to be said. He stands on the grass verge and shines his torch into the undergrowth. There's nothing there. So he shines his torch up the lane instead, to where they're all situated. This anomalous group of toading volunteers. These unusual people. Talking. Sharing hot drinks. Laughing.

This is what it's about, he thinks. *This is what it's really about.*

As if on cue, Dawn takes a flask from her bag. She unscrews the lid and offers the flask in his direction. He holds the cups and Dawn pours the coffee. He watches the steam flower from the coffee cup and how she pours the coffee and he smiles.

He sips the scalding coffee, enjoys the bitter, refreshing taste. He watches Dawn doing the same until she turns to face him, then he looks away.

'Listen,' she says.

He does. And wonders what she means, what he's listening for. Then he hears. The qwark-qwark of toads in the woodland. A curious sound. An under-sound. That grows in volume as he tunes in on it. On them.

'It's the males you can hear,' says Dawn. 'They're the ones making all the noise.'

He nods.

'Seeking a mate,' she says.

'Good for them,' he says. He hands her his coffee cup. He turns towards the torches bobbing in the dark lane.

'I need to answer my own call,' he says. 'It must be the cold. Or the coffee.'

He wanders along the lane, locates Derek with his torch and clipboard.

'Straight through the kitchen into the hall, first door on the right,' says Derek. 'How are you getting on?'

'Grand,' he says. 'Grand. We can hear them, so we know they're there.'

'Oh they're there alright,' says Derek. 'They're always there.'

A set of shelves in the warm hallway. Books about toads. Books and more books. Scientific journals. An illustrated copy of *The Wind in the Willows*. Folklore too. A dozen or so perfectly formed stones on display. He looks at them, feels compelled to touch them.

'Toadstones,' says a voice. Derek's wife, Julie. Descending the stairs. 'Derek's a toad enthusiast, as you've probably gathered. He loves all things Toad.'

'Sorry,' he says. 'I was just –'

'No need to apologise,' says Julie. 'They're there to be enjoyed. Only don't drop them.

They're quite valuable, in a Derek sort of way.'

He picks one up in his fingers. Shiny. Polished. Smooth to the touch. Like obsidian. Like tourmaline. And he feels something. An energy. Or he thinks he does. For a second. And then he dismisses it, returns the stone to the shelf.

Julie smiles. He smiles back.

But it preoccupies him all night, this stone, preoccupies him as he stands in the dark lane with Dawn, listening to the toads but not seeing them, an army awakened, it seems, but not yet on the move.

And so he talks to Dawn. To distract himself. To prevent his mind from lingering on such things, talks about the past, his ties to the place. And hers (an ex-resident). And who she is (divorced, two grown children). What brings her to a dark lane in the earliest intimations of Spring to oversee toad migration from one place to another.

'A nurse,' she says. 'Nurturing comes natural, I guess. Always has.'

And then she says 'It's my day off tomorrow. I might go for a walk. Such lovely weather.'

'Fool's Spring,' he says.

'Is that what they call it?' she asks.

He shrugs.

'Want to join me?' she asks.

He doesn't know what to say, what to do. It's been such a long time since…

'Okay,' he says.

'I'll meet you in the pub car park,' she says. 'At one. We can head off from there. That's what I do. Just a circuit. An hour or two.'

'Derek's got all these stones,' he says. 'Toadstones.'

She opens her mouth to reply, then her eyes dart towards the undergrowth.

'There's one,' says Dawn, breaking away. 'And another. Two of them together.'

He turns his torch beam to hers, locates the two toads, side by side on the edge of the asphalt.

'Best get to it,' she says.

She approaches the toads, lifts one up. He does the same.

The toad sits in the flat of his gloved palm. Squat. Heavily built. A dull brown. He covers it with his other hand. Just as Dawn instructs. They carry the toads across the lane and place them in the undergrowth. One hop and they're gone.

'They look very happy, Julie and Derek. Don't you think?' she asks. 'Very satisfied. Very connected.'

'Very,' he says, because it's all he can think to say.

When it's time to quit they gather again, share numbers, sizes, stories of toads. Then they're making away. In ones and twos. In little units.

'What did you think of Dawn?' asks his mother.

'So that's your game,' he says.

'I thought –' says his mother.

'You thought…' he says.

His father raises an eyebrow, the way his father does.

'Come for your lunch again tomorrow,' says his mother.

'Not tomorrow,' he says. 'I'm busy tomorrow.'

When he arrives at the bungalow the next morning the agent is waiting for him. He walks across the uninspiring gravel, shakes the agent's hand. There are no rose bushes, no borders in which they might grow, but the old bungalow is still there. He can feel its presence beneath these curious, characterless additions, these dead, bolted-on spaces. The living room induces a rush of familiarity. The corner where the TV used to stand. The fireplace he used to sit in front of. He remembers the coal scuttle. The poker. The shovel. The tongues. The fireguard that sat on the hearth. He remembers the smell of the fire, the bright yellow flames. These things come rushing at him. In the master bedroom, he recalls his grandparents' bed, the heavy wooden furniture, catches the scent of lavender where there surely is no scent.

He follows the agent outdoors. The garage is still there. The old brick coal shed is still there. But his grandfather's wooden sheds are gone. The apple tree is gone. There's no vegetable patch. No greenhouse. As there did. As there used to be.

The view from the end of the garden is the same though. He surveys the fields beyond, stubble now, recalls the fields full of golden corn in high summer, recalls his grandmother hoisting him on the wall to watch the combine harvesters in Autumn. Remembers the dust and debris. The noise. Him covering his ears. His grandmother's olive-skinned arms holding him steady, holding him in place. And everything was in place then, wasn't it? Everything identifiable. Everything set. And inevitably not set. Because his grandmother had died, of course. And his grandfather had followed. And the bungalow had passed out of the family. And now here he is, all of these years later, with the possibility of bringing it all back. But he won't do it. He will only think about doing it and imagine doing it and not do it. As is his way. As is the way with everything that does not, in the end, come to pass.

'How was the viewing?' asks Dawn.

'Strange,' he says. 'I probably shouldn't have done it. But it's done now.'

They exit the pub car park, amble through the village in the direction of the sloping village green. It's a pleasant afternoon. A pleasant way to spend an afternoon. And he tells himself as much, that it's pleasant, that there are still pleasures to be had, that it just requires a certain openness, a certain willingness on his part. So pleasant that when they pass the quarry he leads her through the gap in the fence, down into the bottom. She reaches out a hand to balance herself, places it, briefly, on his shoulder and he feels her hand on his shoulder and steadies himself against the slope.

'I used to come here as a boy,' he says.

'Just boys?' she asks. 'Or boys and girls?'

She smiles a playful smile.

'Just boys,' he says.

He bends down, picks up a stone, turns the stone over in his palm.

'Echinoid,' he says. '*Hemicidaris grimaultensis*.'

She looks at it.

'What's that then?' she asks.

'Sea urchin.'

'Around here?'

'From the Jurassic,' he says. 'You know, *Jurassic Park*.'

'Good film,' she says.

She takes out her phone.

'Let me take a photo,' she says.

He holds up the stone and she snaps away.

'That's nice,' she says and shows it to him. 'The stone's not bad either.'

He smiles an awkward smile, leads her out of the quarry, up the hill to the pond.

'I'm going to dredge it,' he says. 'Before I go home.'

'Good for you,' she says.

'Someone should do it, so why not me?' he says.

'Precisely,' she says.

He stands there looking at the pond, thinks about the work that needs to be done, what he's going to need to do it. Then they head back towards the car park, the two of them. He looks at her and she notices him looking.

'Time for a drink?' she asks, gesturing towards the pub doorway.

'I've got to go to town,' he says.

'I'll see you at toading then,' she says, and then she drives away.

He parks at the DIY store, makes his way inside. He's not been in the place five minutes when a bloke approaches him. A stranger. No, a familiar face he can't quite place.

'Julian Balchin?' asks the bloke. He hesitates. Uncertain. Unsure.

'Andy Street,' says the bloke. Then he says, 'Bloody hell, Julian Balchin.'

'Andy,' he says. And he almost remembers. He stands there in the aisle.

'I haven't seen you for years,' says Andy Street. 'Years and years.'

'No,' he says.

'Married?'

'No, not married.'

'Kids?'

'No kids.'

Andy Street puffs out his cheeks, looks somewhere else for a moment. And then he says, 'Keeping busy?'

'Aye, keeping busy.'

Andy Street looks down the aisle to where a woman is standing.

'Duty calls,' he says.

'Aye,' he says.

And then Andy Street is gone.

He buys some rope, a rake, buys a scalpel too, and a plastic chopping board. Back at the annexe he sits on the bed, props his head up with a pillow. His back aches. His neck is stiff. He guesses it's the night in the lane. Or it's psychosomatic, a tightening caused by anxiety, his over-active imagination.

He presses his fingers into his armpit, checks for swelling, copies what the doctor did. He thinks about Andy Street. Old friendships. Passing acquaintances. That a man could become obsolete in his own life and no longer of any use to it. That such things could simply happen without agency. And that a body might recognise such things and duly begin its own process of decommissioning.

He closes his eyes. And sleeps. In a dream, he plucks a dead toad from the tarmac and lifts it in front of him, carries it to Derek and Julie's kitchen, takes the chopping board and the scalpel and cuts into the toad's head just behind the eyes. In a dream, Derek and Julie are smiling. Dawn is there. His parents are watching through the window. But there is no toadstone, or if there is, he is unable to locate it.

'The toad has to be living', says a voice. 'The toad has to be alive'.

I could do it, he thinks, in waking sleep. It would be wrong, but I could do it.

In the morning he trudges up to the pond with the gear, ties the rake to the rope, drags the rake across the surface of the pond, drags the weed and algae from the water, drags and drags and piles the weed at the pond's edge. He cuts the overhanging branches away, clears a swim, then another, imagines two boys fishing on a weekend afternoon. He stays there all day, clearing a route through to the pond from the world beyond.

When evening arrives, he heads out to the lane, to Dawn and the others, spends the hours locating toads and moving toads from one side of the lane to the other. Occasionally he touches the scalpel in his jacket pocket. Occasionally he touches his breast. And occasionally he examines the toads for a hard lump just behind their eyes.

Derek wanders over with his clipboard. They share figures, the numbers of toads they've helped in their quest to reach the pond.

'Someone's been up there,' says Derek. 'Left a right mess.'

Later, he stands in Derek's hallway again. He can hear the flushing toilet and the members of the toading group shouting their goodbyes before heading away. He stares at the books and paraphernalia and the little cluster of stones. Then, guiltily, shockingly, barely aware of himself, he picks up a stone, the one from before, and drops it into his pocket. And it sings to him, this stone. He is certain he can hear it singing.

He meets his parents in the lane. 'I'm heading home,' he says.

'Already?' asks his mum.

'Something's come up at work,' he says.

'Give us a call when you get there,' says his father.

'I will,' he says.

'We worry about you,' says his mum.

He smiles.

'It's okay,' he says. 'I'm okay.'

His father turns and walks over to their car, opens the driver's door. His mother hesitates.

'If anything happens to your father or I, everything is in the back bedroom,' she says. 'In the drawer.'

'Mum,' he says.

'Well, you have to talk about these things,' she says.

'Okay, Mum,' he says. 'Okay.'

She leans forward and kisses him. 'See you, love,' she says.

He watches his mother get into the car and he watches them drive away. They wave and he waves back. And then he walks to his own car, where Dawn is waiting.

'Safe drivly,' she says. He laughs.

'About those toadstones,' she says. 'You can get them online. I've been reading up. It says they have healing properties. It says they can bring a person health and happiness. I could get you one. If you like.'

'I don't suppose it would change much,' he says, feeling in his pocket, feeling the warmth emanating from the stone trapped inside.

'You never know,' she says. 'Look at Julie and Derek.'

She walks down the lane and gets in her car. When she passes him she pulls over.

'I might call you,' she says. 'Visit you some time. What do you think?'

He nods.

'I suppose you could,' he says.

'It's a deal then,' she says.

And then there's just him in the lane. He opens his car door and drops into the driving seat, sits in his car in the dark lane. He watches the last set of taillights disappear and then he sits there for a while longer. He searches up 'Toadstones' on his phone. The button-shaped teeth of Lepitodes. Not from toads at all. But still he wonders. Still he allows himself to imagine. He presses his palm against his breast, examines himself, feels a presence beneath his palm and something beating there. And then he thinks about the drive home, what might be waiting for him on the doormat, of hospital gowns and plain walled rooms and nurses who make saucy jokes.

When the lights go out in the railway cottage, he opens his car door and steps back into the lane.

He heads to the pond, guiding himself by the moonlight, struggling slowly, ungainly up the rise, following his instinct until he feels the pond to one side of him and catches the moonlight on the freshly cleared water. He hears the toads calling, the long flatulent sounds of the toads, an ever-growing mass of toads. He feels a thousand eyes upon him. A thousand eyes and then ten thousand and he sits on the bank amongst them.

He reaches into his pocket, opens his mouth and places the toadstone under his tongue. He thinks of Julie and Derek, thinks of his father, imagines a visit from Dawn.

That the toadstone might really be singing to him. That all things might be mended. That he might flop into the water, submerge himself, and rise to the surface amongst a plenitude of bulbous eyes.

And watch. And wait for something to happen. And be ready for it.

By the far bank, he spots a larger toad, a huge toad, far bigger than the rest. Behind its eyes is a great tumorous swelling. For a long while, the toad sits there on the bank and then, emphatically, it plops into the water where it's swamped by a quantity of smaller toads. He watches the toads churning and writhing in the water, a gelatinous mass of limbs and bodies, and he knows the larger toad is a female and the smaller, male toads are fighting each other to attach themselves to her and that in the end one will win and remain there, grasped in a tight embrace against her until their coupling is over. And he understands in that moment, though in truth he has always known, how he's never held on tightly enough.

Maykopsky District, Adyghe Oblast

Richard Smyth

14-05-1949

Arrival of Comrade SHIRIKOV by mule at the Belaya camp, 125 km west of Makhoshepolyana (see Appendix 5.2). Appeared travel-stained but in good health. Speech of welcome by Partkom Secretary Comrade MIRSKY (see Appendix 1.16.9). Comrade SHIRIKOV swiftly established cordial relations with local populace. Nikolay Mikhaylovich NIKITIN, a military veteran (20th Rifle Division, 1940-45) and hunter not known to be politically active, is engaged as guide for a fee of SR3. After dinner, Comrade SHIRIKOV bathed and retired early.

15-05-1949

At sunrise Comrade SHIRIKOV and Comrade NIKITIN travelled by horse south-west into the forested hills. Comrade SHIRIKOV carried surveying equipment and specialist botany apparatus. He was seen to consult a book later identified as Comrade GULYANOV's *Birds of the Northwestern Caucasus* (1927). During the journey, the two men ate sandwiches and drank vodka. They appeared companionable. At 11:00, they dismounted and made makeshift camp in an area of mixed woodland. Comrade SHIRIKOV was briefly excited by the sight of a plant later identified as the yellow spring gentian (*Gentiana oshtenica*). During the afternoon Comrade SHIRIKOV explored the forest, taking copious notes in a blue-jacketed journal of Finnish manufacture. Comrade NIKITIN smoked tobacco and played grand-patience. Shortly before sunset he fed and watered the horses while Comrade SHIRIKOV cooked mushrooms and onion over the campfire. The two men drank and talked for some time before retiring at midnight to their tents. From what could be heard of their conversation it concerned women, forestry, hunting, leatherwork, seafood, and the Great Stalin Plan for the Transformation of Nature.

16-05-1949

Comrade SHIRIKOV was absent from the camp at daybreak. He was located shortly after 09:00 in the upper limbs of a Nordmann fir (*Abies nordmanniana*), deploying binoculars believed to be of military issue. On return to camp, he spoke enthusiastically to Comrade NIKITIN of shelterbelts and intercropping. Comrade NIKITIN appeared listless. Later he was seen vomiting into a bog myrtle (*Myrica gale*). At 15:00 the men struck camp and returned to Belaya.

17-05-1949

Comrade SHIRIKOV spent the day in his headquarters, apparently writing up his notes and preserving cuttings from the forest expedition. Following consultation with Captain of State Security MARIN it was decided that Comrade SHIRIKOV should be engaged covertly in conversation the following day.

18-05-1949

On emerging from his headquarters at 06:00, purportedly with the intention of listening to the dawn chorus of the birds, Comrade SHIRIKOV was approached by a covert operative and asked his business in Maykopsky District.

SHIRIKOV: I am a functionary of the Main Administration of Field-Protective Afforestation. They have sent me here to inspect and assess the composition and condition of the forest steppe, with a view to the establishment of plantations – shelterbelts, you see – on the steppe north of here. What a lucky fellow I am!

Comrade SHIRIKOV then initiated conversation on the subject of Dawn Clouded Yellows (the covert operative having persuasively adopted the identity of an amateur entomologist specialising in Lepidoptera). The conversation ended when Comrade SHIRIKOV gave a sudden start. He was asked what had occasioned his surprise.

SHIRIKOV: I'm damned if that wasn't the call of Krüper's Nuthatch (*Sitta Krueperi*)!

Comrade SHIRIKOV then departed at speed, headed for nearby trees.

19-05-1949

Having been observed making preparations with Comrade NIKITIN for an expedition, Comrade

SHIRIKOV was approached by a covert operative who offered to accompany the men on their journey. Comrade NIKITIN was heard to make a remark of lewd character. He was sharply rebuked by Comrade SHIRIKOV. Comrade SHIRIKOV then described the proposed expedition as 'rather dull work'.

SHIRIKOV: We are to travel northward to the steppe. We will spend three days (NIKITIN: Three [expletive] days!) taking soil samples and meteorological readings. It will, you see, be no pleasure outing.

Comrade SHIRIKOV was asked to characterise the purpose of the work.

SHIRIKOV: The famine of '46 drove thousands to their graves. In the countryside of the Ukraine men pillaged the cemeteries for meat. This cannot happen again. Look to the United States. Look to their Mister Roosevelt. Twenty-two million trees in eight years. The Great Plains Shelterbelt. An end to soil erosion.

Comrade SHIRIKOV was asked how he came by such detailed statistics.

SHIRIKOV: Why, I keep in close contact with silviculturalists around the world.

While Comrade SHIRIKOV continued his preparations, this information was relayed as a matter of high priority to Captain of State Security MARIN.

Later in the day Comrade SHIRIKOV was persuaded to allow the covert operative to accompany him and Comrade NIKITIN to the steppe. Comrade NIKITIN remained unconvinced.

20-05-1949

The party departed for the steppe at daybreak. The weather was bright and cold, and the wind blew from the west. Comrade NIKITIN led the way on a mule he named Mudakin. Sometimes the party kept to defined tracks. At other times, they travelled cross-country. Comrade NIKITIN seemed fond of saying: 'A short-cut! I promise. A fine [expletive] short-cut!' At 08:30 he took his first drink from an unmarked bottle. Conversation was desultory. Comrade SHIRIKOV seemed engrossed in the study of the arable farmland through which the party travelled. By noon he had gathered some 35 soil samples. Progress was necessarily slow.

At 16:45 the party passed a stunted hornbeam (*Carpinus caucasica*). It was the last tree they would see all day.

At 17:00 Comrade SHIRIKOV pointed to the sky.

NIKITIN: A plane! A Polikarpov Po-2 if I am any judge.

SHIRIKOV: You are no judge at all, Nikitin. Your eyeballs are pickled. It is a lesser-spotted eagle (*Aquila pomarine*). See, it is headed north, for the summer.

NIKITIN: Damn thing looks like a plane from here.

SHIRIKOV: Besides, you lumphead, the Polikarpov Po-2 has not been seen since the war ended.

NIKITIN: I have seen them dusting crops.

SHIRIKOV: What a fine fellow. A fine fellow.

This last observation alluded to the eagle and not to Comrade NIKITIN. It was noted that Comrade

SHIRIKOV appears on all points to be an unusually well-informed individual.

The party made camp on a south-facing escarpment. Rations of cold sausage and adulterated bread were shared. A little vodka was drunk. SHIRIKOV worked on his researches while the daylight lasted. The covert operative feigned perusal of Comrade BIELSOV's *Moths of the USSR and Adjacent Countries* (1940). NIKITOV sang coarse military ballads and before the party retired for the evening made a series of lewd suggestions to the covert operative. Note was taken.

21-05-1949

Comrade NIKITIN gathered plover eggs for breakfast. Comrade SHIRIKOV expressed sympathy for the mother-bird but ate his omelette hungrily.

The party travelled east-north-east until shortly before noon, when camp was made in the open grassland and Comrade SHIRIKOV embarked on an extensive series of topographical surveys. He travelled swiftly and over considerable distances. He appears an assured horseman. It was not always possible for note to be made of his whereabouts. Comrade NIKITIN, under instruction from SHIRIKOV, spent the day folding paper into envelopes for seedlings. The covert operative assembled a moth-trap, baited with molasses.

Darkness fell before Comrade SHIRIKOV had returned.

NIKITIN: He is a canny fellow right enough, but this is deceptive country. Here is much the same as there. Even a canny clever fellow might lose his way and not find it again.

The operative expressed confidence in Comrade SHIRIKOV's navigation skills and predicted his imminent return.

NIKITIN: Aye, but what if he doesn't, eh? What then? I'll tell you what then. It's just me and thee and the steppe. The butterflies and the bees and thee and me, my pet.

The covert operative maintained close surveillance of the dark grasslands. Birds were heard to call from the west.

NIKITIN: It will be a cold night.

In fact, the weather was mild.

At 20:23 the light of a lantern was observed on the northern horizon. It was seen to be moving toward the camp. Soon it could be discerned that the lantern was carried by a man on horseback.

Comrade NIKITIN yelled across the steppe.

NIKITIN: Shirikov, you [expletive]! How you worried us.

Comrade SHIRIKOV rode into the light of the campfire and leapt from his horse. He appeared tired but unharmed.

SHIRIKOV: Feed and water this fine beast, Nikitin. A splendid evening! Do you hear the partridges calling? What is this, a moth-trap? What fun! Why, we must light the lamp and see what comes along. Matches, Nikitin, matches!

As Comrade SHIRIKOV went to work deftly with paraffin, matches and lamp he was asked about his day's work.

SHIRIKOV: I must have ridden a hundred kilometres. Dry work, really, terribly dry: the mapping of elevations, the measurement of moisture and wind-speed, the sampling of soils (this unceasing sampling of soils!). Terribly dry and yet, Comrade – the wildflower scents, the rippling of the wind in the grass, as though the steppe were a beast stirring from sleep, the calls of storks high overhead, the space, the sky, the air – why, it all makes one feel a fortunate fellow indeed.

The lamp was lit. Drinks were poured. There was a smell of warming molasses. The campfire was allowed to peter.

The covert operative pressed for further details regarding Comrade SHIRIKOV's findings.

SHIRIKOV: Oh, it will all be in my report. I have no appetite to speak of it tonight. Besides, look! Someone is coming.

A moth had flown into the globe of light made by the moth-trap lamp. It flew erratically in orbit around the trap.

SHIRIKOV: What is he, Comrade? He is a handsome little thing.

The covert operative suggested that the insect was the Pease Blossom (*Periphanes delphinii*) and met with no disagreement. It was unclear whether this reflected a correct identification or the good manners of Comrade SHIRIKOV. Later scrutiny of Comrade BIELSOV's volume was inconclusive.

NIKITIN: He's getting away.

SHIRIKOV: Molasses and lamplight are nothing to him. Love is what he seeks.

NIKITIN: Slim pickings out here, boy.

SHIRIKOV: Let him go. Let him continue with his search. Let us wish him good fortune.

The moth was soon out of sight. Soon afterwards the party retired.

22-05-1949

The party breakfasted on bacon, onion and black tea. Comrade NIKITIN voiced his intent to spend the morning hunting for Great Bustard (*Otis tarda*).

SHIRIKOV: You will have no luck, Nikitin. We are south and west of the bird's range.

NIKITIN: There will be no roast bustard-meat for you, Comrade, when I return home with a bagful.

The badinage of the two men, though irreverent, remained broadly good-natured.

Comrade SHIRIKOV fell into thoughtful silence while assembling his surveying apparatus for the day ahead. On being questioned, he replied that he had 'been thinking'.

NIKITIN: A dangerous business!

SHIRIKOV: I can see the trees. In my mind's eye. A great rich tapestry of trees tied like a belt across the steppe. I see that it must be done – the land must be cultivated, the topsoil preserved, the winds diverted or diminished – but then there is this question of *how* it is done.

It was asserted by the covert operative that the researches of Comrade LYSENKO had surely established definitively the optimal process of steppe afforestation. Seedlings are planted in small groups and work collectively to combat weeds and pests. Crop plants – winter wheat, flax, alfalfa – will aid the little trees in their struggle. The trees assist one another until the time comes for the lesser saplings to cede to the greater. This new principle of botanical science, the operative said, is central to the Great Stalin Plan for the Transformation of Nature.

Here Comrade NIKITIN burst intemperately into the conversation.

NIKITIN: The Plan is [expletive] and Lysenko is a [expletive] fraud.

SHIRIKOV: [calmly, addressing the operative] You seem to know a terrific amount about it, Comrade.

Note was taken. The query was deflected.

Comrade SHIRIKOV invited the covert operative to accompany him in his surveying.

SHIRIKOV: It will be less strenuous than yesterday. That is, if you would not sooner be butterflying? You have such a handsome net – a good cane grip, silk mesh, I envy you your outfitter – and I have hardly seen you put it to use.

The operative explained convincingly that there would be ample time for both.

By 10:00 the operative and Comrade SHIRIKOV were out of sight of the camp. The day was overcast but not dull. Hares raced through the feathergrass (*Stipa pennata*). Comrade SHIRIKOV drew the operative's attention to a serpent eagle flying across the wind. Shortly before noon he stopped his horse and invited the operative to imagine a forest where at the time there was only grass.

SHIRIKOV: It seems madness, does it not, Comrade? A woodland of oak and beech, hornbeam and larch – here! Here where there is not a tree in sight. Where a man might see clear to the church towers of Rostov simply by standing up in his saddle. But it can be done, I think. I think it can be done. A woodland of birdsong. Of scampering squirrels and martens. Men will come here to coppice the young trees or to hunt deer and bear and wolf – and none of your scrawny steppe-wolves, either. Mothers will bring their children to gather nuts and play in the groves of bluebell and wood anemone. Lovers might come here, eh? The air will be sweet. Can you imagine it, Comrade? Can you see it?

Note was taken of Comrade SHIRIKOV's ardent expression and emotional tone of voice.

The operative civilly reminded Comrade SHIRIKOV that the purpose of the Great Stalin Plan for the Transformation of Nature was primarily agricultural.

SHIRIKOV: But of course! That too, Comrade. That too.

Note was taken.

A trumpeting noise was heard in the west. As though in response to a signal Comrade SHIRIKOV spurred his horse. The operative followed. At 12:23 a shallow river (see Appendix 5.3) was reached, at which Comrade SHIRIKOV pulled up, and gestured to the opposing bank.

SHIRIKOV: Demoiselle cranes (*Grus virgo*).

Eight tall birds with silver bodies and black-and-white plumes were dancing on the far bank of the river. Up they leapt and down they stooped. Their broad wings billowed like fine cloaks. The sunshine was pale.

Comrade SHIRIKOV watched in apparent rapture.

SHIRIKOV: Better than the damn Kirov, eh.

The operative offered no reply.

Survey work occupied most of the rest of the day (see Report of Officer P.P. Shirikov [incomplete], 23/05/1949).

23-05-1949

Breakfast was taken hastily as there was much to be done.

NIKITIN: You will run those horses into the ground.

SHIRIKOV: It is only one day more, Nikitin.

NIKITIN: This [expletive] fool's errand has already taken two days too long.

Comrade SHIRIKOV and the covert operative rode due north in bright sunshine. Wildflower meadows seemed to unfurl beneath the blue skies. Comrade SHIRIKOV demonstrated commendable mastery of plant identification. It was noted that Comrade SHIRIKOV is an individual of remarkable mental and physical gifts.

SHIRIKOV: It is funny to think of some hairy fellow hoeing weeds from his alfalfa here a few years hence.

It was observed that according to Comrade LYSENKO the hairy fellow might take his ease while the seedling oaks worked in partnership to drive the weeds away.

SHIRIKOV: Let us not speak of that now.

It was remarked by the operative that there might be said to be a sort of beauty in the steppe despite its lack of productivity.

SHIRIKOV: There is indeed a beauty in its uselessness.

OPERATIVE: It seems a dangerous thing to say.

SHIRIKOV: Perhaps, but who is to overhear us, a hundred kilometres from anywhere?

Note was taken of an ironic note in Comrade SHIRIKOV's voice.

OPERATIVE: You said that lovers might come here. Once it has been forested.

SHIRIKOV: All lovers crave a shady bower, unless – God forbid it! – poetry has misled me.

OPERATIVE: It seems to me, Comrade, that lovers might just as well come to a steppe as to a forest.

SHIRIKOV: I suppose one place might be as good as another.

OPERATIVE: It is good enough, after all, for the love-dances of the Demoiselle cranes.

SHIRIKOV: And for other love-dances, too.

To the south, from far across the steppe, six rifle-shots sounded in a pattern of one-two, two-one.

Comrade SHIRIKOV calmed his horse and then, taking binoculars from his pocket, scanned the southern horizon.

SHIRIKOV: I see nothing. It must be that happy fool Nikitin, blazing away at what he fancies are bustards. They will be chukars, no doubt. But we were saying, Comrade?

OPERATIVE: You ought not call me Comrade.

SHIRIKOV: Why, then what am I to call you?

OPERATIVE: You ought not call me anything.

SHIRIKOV: You do not wish me to call you by your name?

OPERATIVE: What one wishes is a secondary concern.

Comrade SHIRIKOV looked up and pointed to a pair of large raptors flying north-west.

SHIRIKOV: Imperial eagles, I think. I have not seen them before. You are NKVD, of course?

The operative offered no reply.

SHIRIKOV: You are certainly no lepidopterist. Pease Blossom, my foot. Am I condemned? I do not recall having spoken loosely until today.

The operative offered no reply.

SHIRIKOV: I tell you, Comrade, that I *am* condemned, one way or another.

Note was taken of a certain pain in the eyes of Comrade SHIRIKOV.

The operative explained to SHIRIKOV that a particular pre-arranged signal was to have been given should the unfortunate necessity have arisen of placing Comrade SHIRIKOV or any other individual in state custody. NKVD officers had followed the party from the camp at Belaya and were stationed nearby in a state of readiness.

SHIRIKOV: And you have given the signal, I suppose?

OPERATIVE: I have not.

SHIRIKOV: Well, then, perhaps –

The operative explained that the pre-arranged signal was a series of six gunshots, in a pattern of one–two, two–one.

SHIRIKOV: Nikitin!

OPERATIVE: I did not know.

SHIRIKOV: They will be waiting for me at the camp.

OPERATIVE: He saw that you doubted Lysenko.

Comrade SHIRIKOV spoke briefly but volubly in respect of Comrade LYSENKO's work and character.

OPERATIVE: Run. Your horse will carry you to Rostov, perhaps.

SHIRIKOV: But you would be made to pay for the loss, Comrade.

To the east the Demoiselle cranes were heard to hoot. Comrade SHIRIKOV turned his horse into the sun. He spoke the name of Comrade NIKITIN and smiled.

SHIRIKOV: See, Comrade, how cleverly we work together to pluck the weeds from our midst.

The horse of the operative was also turned toward the sun. The two long shadows were seen to touch and so become a single shadow.

This concludes the report of Lieutenant of State Security M.A. Pavlichenko. It may be construed as constituting a letter of resignation. It will be sealed in a seedling envelope and deposited in the river where the Demoiselle cranes dance.

About the Authors

Born in Belfast in 1981, **Lucy Caldwell** is the author of four novels, including the forthcoming *These Days* (Faber, 2022), several stage plays and radio dramas and two collections of short stories: *Multitudes* and *Intimacies*. She is also the editor of *Being Various: New Irish Short Stories*. Awards include the Rooney Prize for Irish Literature, the George Devine Award for Most Promising Playwright, the Dylan Thomas Prize, the Imison Award, and a Major Individual Artist Award from the Arts Council of Northern Ireland. A former fellow of the Royal Literary Fund and the Seamus Heaney Centre at Queen's, a Visiting Fellow at Goldsmith's, she was also elected a Fellow of the Royal Society of Literature in 2018. In 2021, *The Sunday Times* proclaimed her 'One of Ireland's most essential writers.'

Rory Gleeson is a novelist, playwright, and screenwriter. He studied Psychology at Trinity College Dublin before earning further degrees from The University of Manchester, Oxford University, and UEA. His writing has featured in *The Irish Times, Sunday Miscellany, Far Off Places Magazine* and *Granta*. He was the Burgess Fellow for Fiction at The University of Manchester in 2019 and was awarded a Literature Bursary by Arts Council Ireland in 2020. His debut novel *Rockadoon Shore* was published by John Murray Press in 2017.

Georgina Harding is the author of six novels, including *Harvest* (Bloomsbury, 2021), *The Spy Game* (2009), which was shortlisted for the Encore Award, and *Painter of Silence* (2012), which was shortlisted for the Orange Prize for Fiction. Georgina Harding lives in London and on a farm in the Stour Valley, Essex.

Born in Lincolnshire, **Danny Rhodes** is the author of several short stories and novels, including *Asboville* (Maia Press, 2006) which was adapted for BBC Films by Nick Leather, and selected as a Waterstones Booksellers Paperback of the Year. His other works include *Soldier Boy* (2009) and *FAN* (2014), a novel grounded in his experience as a Nottingham Forest supporter at the Hillsborough disaster in 1989.

Richard Smyth is a writer, critic and author of *The Woodcock* (Fairlight Books, 2021). His work has appeared in *The Guardian, The New Statesman* and *The Times Literary Supplement*, and he is the author of five books of non-fiction. He lives in Bradford, West Yorkshire, with his family.

About the BBC National Short Story Award with Cambridge University

The BBC National Short Story Award is one of the most prestigious for a single short story and celebrates the best in home-grown short fiction. The ambition of the award, which is now in its sixteenth year, is to expand opportunities for British writers, readers and publishers of the short story, and honour the UK's finest exponents of the form. The award is a highly regarded feature within the literary landscape with a justified reputation for genuinely changing writers' careers.

James Lasdun secured the inaugural award in 2006 for 'An Anxious Man'. Jumping to 2012, when the Award expanded internationally for one year to mark the London Olympics, the Bulgarian writer Miroslav Penkov was victorious with his story 'East of the West'. We've seen a trend towards writers who are 'earlier' in their writing journeys coming through to the shortlist and winning in recent years. Following her win in 2018, Ingrid Persaud signed with Rogers Coleridge White literary agency after being courted by multiple agents, and went on to sell her debut novel *Love After Love* to Faber & Faber in a seven-way auction. 2019 winner Jo Lloyd also signed with an agent and published her first collection of short stories. In 2020, four-time nominated Sarah Hall won the Award for the second time with 'The Grotesques'. The first double win in the Award's history, the judges praised Hall for her extraordinary, layered and masterful writing and cited her double win as 'recognition of her standing as the country's foremost writer of short stories'. Other alumni include Lionel Shriver, Zadie Smith, Hilary Mantel, Jon McGregor, Rose Tremain and William Trevor.

The winning author receives £15,000, and four further shortlisted authors £600 each. All five shortlisted stories are broadcast on BBC Radio 4 along with interviews with the writers.

In 2015, to mark the National Short Story Award's tenth anniversary, the BBC Young Writers' Award was launched in order to inspire the next generation of short story writers, to raise the profile of the form with a younger audience, and provide an outlet for their creative labours. The teenage writers shortlisted for the award have their stories recorded by professional actors and broadcast, plus they are interviewed on-air and in the media. The winner of the 2020 award was 19-year-old Lottie Mills, from Hertfordshire, with her story 'The Changeling', a story inspired by 'otherhood' and her frustration with 'how difference, especially disability, is represented in fiction.' Lottie was the first young writer who had been previously shortlisted for the award – in 2018 – and gone on to win in a subsequent year.

To inspire the next generation of short story readers, teenagers around the UK are also involved in the BBC National Short Story Award via the BBC Student Critics' Award, which gives selected 16- to 18-year-olds the opportunity to read, listen to, discuss and critique the five stories shortlisted by the judges, and have their say. The students are supported with discussion guides, teaching resources and interactions with writers and judges, for an enriching experience that brings literature to life.

The year 2018 marked the start of an exciting collaboration between the BBC and the University of Cambridge. The University of Cambridge supports all three awards, and hosts a range of short story events at the Institute of Continuing Education, which offers a range of creative writing and English Literature programmes, and curates an exclusive online exhibition of artefacts drawn from the University Library's archive to inspire and intrigue entrants of the Young Writers' Award.

For more information on the awards, please visit www.bbc.co.uk/nssa and www.bbc.co.uk/ywa. You can also keep up-to-date on Twitter via #BBCNSSA, #BBCYWA and #shortstories

Award Partners

BBC Radio 4 is the world's biggest single commissioner of short stories, which attract more than a million listeners. Contemporary stories are broadcast every week, the majority of which are specially commissioned throughout the year.
www.bbc.co.uk/radio4

BBC Radio 1 is the UK's No.1 youth station, targeting 15- to 29-year-olds with a distinctive mix of new music and programmes focusing on issues affecting young people. The station is the soundtrack to young people's lives in the UK and has been for over 50 years.
www.bbc.co.uk/radio1

The mission of the **University of Cambridge** is to contribute to society through the pursuit of education, learning and research at the highest international levels of excellence. To date, 96 affiliates of the University have won the Nobel Prize. Founded in 1209, the University comprises 31 autonomous Colleges, which admit students and provide small-group tuition, and 150 departments, faculties and institutions. Cambridge is a global university. Its 19,000 student body includes 3,700 international students from 120 countries. Cambridge researchers collaborate with colleagues worldwide, and the University has established larger-scale partnerships in Europe, Asia, Africa and America. The BBC National Short Story Award is being supported by the School of Arts and Humanities, Faculties of English and Education, University Library, Fitzwilliam Museum and the new University of Cambridge Centre for Creative Writing which is part of the University of Cambridge's Institute of Continuing Education based at Madingley Hall, which provides a range of courses to members of the public, including English Literature and Creative Writing. More information at www.ice. cam.ac.uk/bbcshortstory

Previous Winners

2020: 'The Grotesques' by Sarah Hall

2019: 'The Invisible' by Jo Lloyd

2018: 'The Sweet Sop' by Ingrid Persaud

2017: 'The Edge of the Shoal' by Cynan Jones

2016: 'Disappearances' by KJ Orr
Runner-up: 'Morning, Noon & Night'
by Claire-Louise Bennett

2015: 'Briar' by Jonathan Buckley
Runner-up: 'Bunny' by Mark Haddon

2014: 'Kilifi Creek' by Lionel Shriver
Runner-up: 'Miss Adele Amidst the Corsets'
by Zadie Smith

2013: 'Mrs Fox' by Sarah Hall
Runner-up: 'Notes from the House Spirits'
by Lucy Wood

2012: 'East of the West' by Miroslav Penkov
Runner-up: 'Sanctuary' by Henrietta Rose-Innes

PREVIOUS WINNERS

2011: 'The Dead Roads' by D W Wilson
Runner-up: 'Wires' by Jon McGregor

2010: 'Tea at the Midland' by David Constantine
Runner-up: 'If It Keeps On Raining'
by Jon McGregor

2009: 'The Not-Dead & the Saved' by Kate
Clanchy
Runner-up: 'Moss Witch' by Sara Maitland

2008: 'The Numbers' by Clare Wigfall
Runner-up: 'The People on Privilege Hill'
by Jane Gardam

2007: 'The Orphan and the Mob' by Julian Gough
Runner-up: 'Slog's Dad' by David Almond

2006: 'An Anxious Man' by James Lasdun
Runner-up: 'The Safehouse' by Michel Faber